High Ridge Range

G·K
Hall
&C⁰.

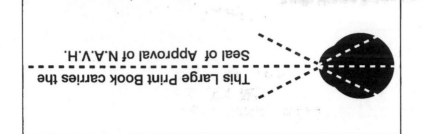

This Large Print Book carries the
Seal of Approval of N.A.V.H.

Also by Lauran Paine
in Large Print:

The Apache Kid
The Arizona Panhandle
The Blue Basin Country
Cache Canon
Custer Meadow
The Devil on Horseback
The General Custer Story
The Grand Ones of San Ildefonso
Greed at Gold River
Homesteaders
The Killer Gun
Lockwood
The Manhunter
Marshal
The Misplaced Psyche
Moon Prairie
Murder Now Pay Later

High Ridge Range

LAURAN PAINE

G.K. Hall & Co. • Thorndike, Maine

Published in 1999 by arrangement with Golden West Literary Agency.

G.K. Hall Large Print Paperback Series.

The text of this Large Print edition is unabridged.
Other aspects of the book may vary from the original edition.

Set in 16 pt. Plantin.

Printed in the United States on permanent paper.

Library of Congress Cataloging-in-Publication Data

Paine, Lauran.
   High ridge range / Lauran Paine.
     p. cm.
   ISBN 0-7838-8792-2 (lg. print : sc : alk. paper)
   1. Large type books. I. Title.
PS3566.A34 H55 1999
813′.54 21—dc21   99-045560

High Ridge Range

One

The New Hand

According to old Bill Burton the high ridge country began in mid-Colorado and did not end until it had crossed over into Mexico, and he had at one time or another ranged cattle over every mile of it, even down over the line into Sonora in Mexico.

He may have been correct; Paul Franklyn had been riding for seventeen days since reaching the high ridge country, coming onto it from the east, from over in Nebraska, and for all he knew, since he had never been south of New Mexico in all his life, Burton's information was right. Nor did he particularly care how far south the high ridge country ran; he was solely concerned with how far *he* had run.

He knew there was a town to the west because he had seen sun bouncing off a turning windmill over there, and some tin rooftops. He also knew, because he had been riding through bunches of them for two days, that there was a big cow outfit east of that town.

Bill Burton was the rangeboss. When Paul had

ridden in sifted over with trail-dust, Bill had been leaning in a wagon-side watching him, had in fact been watching him since one of the riding crew loping in for supper had reported a stranger bound for the yard.

Bill was a wiry man a little below average height, grey as a badger, with blue eyes that missed nothing and which in their weathered, wrinkled setting were calm, stone-steady, and shrewd. Bill was fifty-five and looked seventy. He had been rangeboss for the Weatherford family since he had been twenty-six. He had served under three heads of the absentee Weatherford family, and had been able to get along well with them all.

Bill was a legend in the high ridge range country. He had once married a Crow woman. She had died two years after their son had been born, and the child had followed her before he was seven. Their graves were up a hidden canyon of the far foothills. Bill never mentioned either one of them, but the sixth day after he had hired Paul Franklyn to ride for Weatherford Ranch, and they were hunting a lame bull some-one had reported seeing near a spring in the foot-hills, Bill led out along a redstone ledge to the very edge and sat his horse, gloved hands atop the saddlehorn gazing down into a place where the sun did not touch before eleven in the morning nor after three in the afternoon, and quietly said, "There's my family, Paul. You see those red-rock mounds? The one with the flowers growin' around it — that's my wife. The little one — that's our son."

Paul looked and said nothing. Someone had painstakingly transplanted wild flowers down there. Probably the same person who had carried cement up here to make a little red-rock cross above the pair of graves.

Paul knew about death and graves, but at eighteen that was about all he knew of those things. When they reined back to look for the bull — which they never found — Bill put a cud of tobacco into his cheek and spoke in a different tone of voice.

"You been on the range a week now, boy, and you know north from south, so startin' tomorrow you're on your own. To start with, see if you can find this bull."

They did not exchange another word for seven miles, which was the distance back to the yard, and that evening after supper Paul went out back to the pole corrals to roll and light a smoke and gaze back where those red-rock ridges showed darkly against the farther-off background of big mountains.

He was still out there when Bud Fisk ambled over from the rear of the big log barn and smiled as he said, "Pretty night. From now on they'll be a little warmer. When I was your age I rode up in eastern Wyoming. It got so cold up there you could hear it." Bud was a rawboned, coppery-coloured man with a hooked nose and a wide, thin mouth which seemed ready to curl into a grin at any moment. He was Bill Burton's tophand and had been for six years. Bud was in his mid-thirties, but he too looked older. They all did if they followed their trade long enough. They all shared another peculiar distinction, if they stayed with saddlebacking long enough, they became not exactly reclusive, but they certainly became private men.

Bud hooked a worn boot over the bottom pole and got comfortable as he went on speaking. "Weatherford's a decent outfit. Maybe because Bill runs it and the owners live in New York." Bud chuckled at that. "A man could do a lot worse than to settle in, and maybe Bill'd keep you through the winter. We always keep a couple extra hands on through."

Paul looked at the amiable, lanky older man. "You been here long?"

"Seven years. Six as the tophand." Bud ranged a long look over the immensity of range country and added a little more. "I'll likely die here. That's fine with me."

Paul continued to regard the tophand, then eventually he turned back to considering the ice-chip stars, the little sickle moon, and what could still be made out of those red-rock bluffs. "I got to go find that lame bull tomorrow," he said, and paused for a long time before also saying, "Did you know Bill's got two graves up in there?"

Bud knew. He and Bill Burton were old, close friends. "Yeah. He showed 'em to you?"

"Yes. We were on a bluff overlooking the

10

canyon. He showed me where they were."

Bud considered the horses in the nearest big pole corral. "He don't do that often. Don't talk about it to him."

"I won't. Bud, I buried my maw and paw."

Fisk cleared his throat. "I guess we all do that sooner or later, boy."

"Yeah — but I never went back to plant flowers."

Bud straightened up. "Someday, Paul. You're young. Someday you will. We better bed down. Four o'clock comes right early, even this spring-time of the year."

The yard was large with log buildings upon both sides of it. The lighted bunkhouse had a small porch with a wooden overhang over it and some chairs out there. The only other lighted building was the cookhouse where they ate. It was diagonally opposite the bunkhouse, about halfway between the barn and bunkhouse. At the extreme southern end of the yard was the owner's main-house. It was large and had a wide veranda completely around it, roofed over and two steps up off the ground. It was dark. It very rarely was not dark at night. When the Weather-fords came west it was usually to vacation for a few weeks, then return to New York. The last time any of them had been on the ranch was almost two years earlier when the clan's patri-arch, old Franklyn Weatherford, had died, and two sons had come west to notify Bill Burton that henceforth as executors, they would receive

11

all letters and reports. That had not seemed to make any difference. As Bill told his tophand, the ranch was only one of the Weatherford holdings, and it probably was the one which made the least profit; that old Franklyn had loved it, but if he hadn't come out of the cow country as a youth to get rich in the east, the family probably would have sold it off long ago.

After being notified that the old man had died, Bill had kept his thoughts private about the future of the outfit, but he had not expected the Weatherfords to keep it, and now almost two years later it was beginning to appear that he had been wrong in his private thoughts; they were keeping it. In their letters to him there had never been a hint of selling out. For Bill Burton, to whom Weatherford Ranch was home, this was a great relief. In more ways than most people imagined Bill's roots were there on the high ridge range country.

He was reading the most recent letter from New York when Bud and the new hand ambled in out of the night. He heard them talking to the other riders through the thin partition which divided his little room as rangeboss from the larger room where the crew bedded down. He stepped to the door, caught the tophand's eye and jerked his head.

Fisk had shed his hat and vest. He entered Bill's room scratching his coarse mane of salt-and-pepper dark hair. Bill pointed to a half-empty bottle on a makeshift dresser. "Get your

12

feet warm," he said, and sat back down at his old table. "I got a letter from back east."

Fisk was weakening the whisky with water from a dipper. "Someone is coming out?"

"No. Well, yeah, someone is coming, but it's a lawyer, not one of the family, and he might not show up until mid-summer."

Bud took his watered whisky to a chair. "Something wrong?"

Bill Burton snorted. "They don't say so. They never tell me anything, just write about what they're figurin' to do. As far as I know, there's nothing wrong *here;* back there, I got no idea what might be wrong."

Bud finished his drink and settled more comfortably into the chair. "What else is on your mind?"

They knew each other very well. Bill put down the letter and gazed over at his tophand. "The new hand's goin' up to look for that lame bull tomorrow."

"Yeah, he told me a while ago out back. You couldn't find him, eh?"

"I didn't really look, Bud. I wanted to ride around a little, figure him out."

Fisk considered the lined, ruddy face through smoky lamplight and said nothing.

Bill arose and got himself one of those glasses of branch-water and whisky. As he returned to his chair, "Eighteen."

Bud still said nothing, but he kept his gaze upon the rangeboss.

Bill drank half the glassful then set it aside. "Same age as my boy would have been."

This time Bud nodded his head. "I know."

"You know anything else about this lad, Bud?"

"Well, he buried his maw and paw back east, and he's got some raw scars inside his head. Otherwise he's good with a horse; we've had worse hands on the ranch."

Bill leaned on the old desk gazing steadily at his tophand. "He's wanted for murder in Nebraska, Bud."

Fisk blinked but otherwise showed no astonishment. He shifted a little in the chair, then said, "How do you know that?"

"I been tryin' to recollect where I saw him before. It came to me this evening at supper. There's a dodger about him on the post office wall in town."

Bud sat a thoughtful length of time in silence, then looked into his empty glass, arose to cross to the table where he made another drink. Then he turned. "What you goin' to do?"

Burton had been wrestling with this same question for hours. "I thought if I rode into town tomorrow, I could find out more. Meanwhile, if he's up in the foothills lookin' for that bull —"

Bud returned to his chair. "Yeah; he'll be away from here. Bill, I've seen how you do things for a long time. I know you pretty well. Listen to me — you got to either haul him up to the sheriff in town, or send him on his way. Wait a minute —

let me finish. I know how old he is and I knew yesterday when you rode out with him you had a sort of image of another young buck who'd be about like him in your mind." Bud drank his glass empty, then said, "Not a murderer, Bill. I don't give a damn how he comes across to you — not a murderer."

Fisk arose and set his glass over on the table, then turned with a soft-sad smile. "Good night."

Outside, probably because it was springtime, a pair of wolves sounded back and forth in the lower mountains, and in that glass-clear air the sound carried for miles. One was a dog-wolf and the other was a bitch-wolf.

Otherwise the land lay softly hushed in all its moonlighted immensity, and Bud Fisk rolled into his blankets, turned his back to the popping old iron wood-stove, and went to sleep. He had been a number of places, had survived a variety of difficulties, and nothing kept him from his sleep when it was time to roll in.

Two

The Three-legged Bull

Bill was gone by the time the riders crossed for breakfast to the cookshack, and that made Bud look concernedly at the ground underfoot as he trooped back from breakfast to rig out his horse for the day.

The four hired hands, besides Bud and Paul Franklyn, left the yard in a bunch, bundled inside their sheep-pelt coats, riding ranch horses with a nubbin under the saddleblanket. But none of them bucked; those men were seasoned rangeriders, they knew when and how to kid a horse out of bucking on a cold morning.

Paul got saddled and led his animal out back before mounting. He was in no hurry. Bud watched him from inside the barn. Whoever had told the new hand about a cold-backed horse in the early morning had taught him well.

Paul turned the horse a few times, then cheeked him and swung up. The horse lined out without so much as a snort. Bud wagged his head. Whoever he had been, he had for a fact taught the lad exactly right.

By the time Bud left the yard the *cosinero* had finished cleaning up after breakfast and came outside on the porch to fling away greasy water. He was a big, flabby man with a warped leg. He waited until he saw the tophand bust over into an easy lope, northward, then hastened back inside to lean far over and plunge a hairy arm into the flour-barrel where he kept his whisky-bottle hidden.

There was not a cloud in the sky, stars shone, but were beginning to bleach out, and it was cold as Paul loped for two miles then walked another mile. It was seven miles from the yard to the foothills, and seven miles back. Unless he found that sore-footed bull by early afternoon he was going to eat a cold supper under the disapproving glare of the cook.

He avoided the hidden canyon where the graves were. The bull was not up there or he and Burton would have seen him the day before.

What he sought, and ultimately found, was a set of tracks left by a heavy critter which had been favouring his left foreleg. There were a lot of tracks up through here, but they did not all belong to an old snorter who was grumpy, and that made trailing him easier.

The tracks seemed to hug the northward hills in the area just before the genuine mountains were reached, and the bull was travelling slowly. Paul was confident. For a rangeman, he was good at reading sign, and this time, when the bull eventually left broken country to graze, he should be visible, now that there was dawnlight to see by.

He found the bull, not by sight but by sound. He was not quite clear of the foothills and had his back to a crumbly rock-slide or otherwise Paul would not have found him alive. There were four big wolves, three in their prime and one old lobo with a white muzzle. The old dog-wolf knew every manoeuvre by heart, but he could not flank the bull because of that crumbly rock. The three younger dog-wolves were baiting the bull, rushing in, snarling to draw him into a charge so the old wolf could hamstring him from behind. But the three-legged bull was no novice either. He looked to be maybe eight years old, which was too old actually for a seed-bull, but many cow outfits did not cull that close, and he had scars from many battles. His head was lowered, his little eyes were bloodshot and his muzzle dripped. He was fighting mad; would fight anything right at this moment including a mounted man. But he had a badly swollen ankle and barely put any weight upon that side as he swung wicked, curved horns from side to side.

How it might have ended was anyone's guess, but Paul left his horse among some jack-pines, yanked loose the tie-down over his gun-handle, and by keeping as much of that crumbly slope between himself and the wolves as he could, began a stalk.

Another time the wolves might not have been that easy to reach, but now they were pressing the bull hard, and in anticipation of ripping him open to fill up on warm meat they did not heed their built-in warning systems until it was too late.

The noise carried too, and that masked Paul's sounds as he came through the crumbly tallis. Then he was ready, peeled off his right-hand glove, leaned to look around where the fight was in progress, then stepped into full view and called out sharply.

The old wolf's hearing was not that good, but the younger wolves heard the call and saw the man at the same time. They froze and that was their final error. Paul's right arm seemed scarcely to dip. Three slamming, thunderous sixgun blasts with less than two seconds between ended it. The big younger wolves were bowled over and flung backwards under impact as though they were rags.

The old white-muzzled wolf recovered from astonishment and would have turned, but Paul called to him. He hesitated, looking directly at the man with the smoking gun in his hand. For about five seconds they stared steadily at each other, then Paul shot the wolf, and this time the big animal simply folded all four legs and dropped straight down, his heart blown to bits.

Paul eyed the fighting-mad bull and was glared back at, but the bull could not charge on three legs. Paul methodically plugged out the empties, pushed in reloads from his belt, leathered the gun and walked over. If it had been wintertime he would have skinned the big wolves. Now, their hair was slipping so the hides were no good.

He turned to face the bull. There was about sixteen hundred pounds of him, and even if he'd had four good legs under him no one was going to drive him anywhere. The little bloodshot eyes glowed malevolently, he still slobbered, and although he raised his head a little, he was still holding it in a position to gore.

Paul rolled and lit a smoke. The bull did not move, but he watched Paul's every move. He was tucked up, probably because he had been unable to graze properly for some time, and as Paul stood there studying the animal he thought the bull had probably been snake-bitten. He could not see the puncture holes, but that was his guess. He'd seen them like this before, sometimes from infected splinters, sometimes from snake-bite. The usual procedure was for two ropers to head and heel the critter and stretch him flat while the third rangeman went in for the doctoring. Paul was alone. The bull might have been drivable before the wolves got him sweating mad, but even then it would have taken a full day to get him seven miles along, and most likely when he got tired of being driven he'd lie down and sull. There was no way to get an animal this large back on his feet if he sulled, but that was not Paul's problem either.

They regarded each other for a long time, until Paul dropped the quirley and ground it out, then the bull, body-heat dropping a little, shifted position slightly and raised his head to look elsewhere, out where the good grass was, and off to his right into the broken country. He abruptly stiffened. Paul turned to follow out the direction the bull was staring, and saw the horseman walking steadily toward him from over to the northeast maybe a mile and a half.

They both watched the rider until Paul recognised him. It was Bud Fisk, and he was poking along in an easy slouch gazing ahead at them. He did not lift a gloved hand in salute. He did not even smile and nod when he got up there, just halted and sat a moment gazing at the dead wolves, and the lame bull. He eventually said, "Where is your horse?"

Paul pointed. "Yonder in the pines."

"Go get him. We'll see what luck we can have at stretching this old cuss out. What's it look like to you?"

"Snake-bite."

Bud nodded, then looked around again. "What was they doin', tryin' to bait him into a charge?"

"Yeah."

Bud continued to look at the dead wolves. "Was there more of them?"

"No. Just these four, and one was darn near as old as I am."

Bud nodded, leaned back to take down his rope, and Paul took this as his cue so he went back for his horse.

By the time Paul returned astride Bud Fisk had made as good an examination of the three-legged bull as he could, and was getting back across leather. In a less crisp tone he said, "I think you're right. It looks like he got snake-bit. How good are you with a rope, Paul?"

"About average, I expect," the younger man replied, taking down his rope and shaking out a small loop for heading.

Bud shook his head. "I'll head, you heel."

They eased up on the bull. He promptly lowered his head in a threatening way, but he could not charge them, so they went still closer, and for someone as seasoned as Bud Fisk roping those wide, stationary horns was as easy as falling off a log.

The bull lunged, flinging up his head, but he could not run, and as he swung away from the rock-slide, hobbling clumsily, Paul snagged both rear legs below the hocks. With four good legs to plant solidly down that big bull would have been a problem to dump, but this was a three-legged bull. He struggled to remain upright, staggered like a drunk man over fifty yards, then went down. Bud was on the ground in a second as he called back to Paul. "Keep your slack."

Bud avoided the threshing horns, flicked open his Barlow knife, leaned down and probed the rope-held swollen foot. There was a hot place which was softer than the surrounding meat. Most of the hair had sloughed off over this place. Bud leaned closer, plunged in the tip of his knife-blade, then turned it to rip crossways as he withdrew the blade. Hot pus boiled out, the bull let go with a great, strangling roar and beat the ground with his head. Bud reached with his free hand to yank loose his head-rope, then he turned and ran back to his horse and sprang across leather.

The bull came up onto all four feet, killing mad, but Bud backed his horse well clear, then waited. The bull made an unsteady attempt to rush him, Bud looked up, and Paul, easing ahead, flipped his slack until his heel-rope came off, and the bull was free.

He stopped his rush as Bud turned and loped around him to meet Paul, then looped his reins, fished out his tobacco-sack and went to work as Paul finished coiling his rope and made it fast to the swells. Then Bud said, "You do all right with a rope."

It was a compliment, about as good a one as any rangeman would ever offer. He lit up and watched the bull go limping out toward open country. "You was right, he'd been snake-bit. There was the two little fang-marks. Well, he won't pester no heifers for a month or two, will he?"

Paul made a thin smile in the direction of the wicked-horned old redback. "I'm glad we could do it. That must have hurt like hell."

Bud sat gazing at the younger man for a long while. "It's only an old range bull."

Paul answered while still watching the bull

23

limp on his way. "That don't matter; he can hurt, an' they can't help themselves."

Bud continued to sit there smoking for a moment or two longer, then jerked his head. "All right. I lent you a hand. Now you can lend me one. I was supposed to find some first-calf heifers over east of here, and when I heard all that shootin' I got curious."

They did not exchange another word as they rode back into the foothills on an easy lope heading toward the mountains, but on an angling, paralleling course.

There was a little more timber over where Bud finally dropped down to a walk and gestured with a gloved hand. "You take it down yonder and I'll stay higher. There's a spring about a mile dead ahead. That's where I was aimin' when I heard the gunfire. They'll likely be over there. If you find 'em, just set there, I'll be along directly."

Paul watched the tophand ride away. There had been something different between them today. Every other time he and the tophand had been together, on the range or at the homeplace, Bud had smiled a lot and had been friendly in an understanding way. Today he had not smiled once, and although he had complimented Paul on the heeling of that old bull he had not sounded quite friendly.

Maybe he was off his feed. It happened with older men. Paul started riding a little southward around the knobs and crumbly-ridges. When he could make out standing trees off on his left a fair distance he guessed that was where the water-hole was, and changed course slightly. He picked up the cattle-smell from a half-mile out, went in behind a landswell, and eased up carefully until he could look down the far side where those trees were.

It looked to be maybe forty or fifty heavy heifers down there, mingling with some wet cows with sassy redback calves at their sides. He knew what Bud would look for, and eased into sight very slowly, never closing the distance, and began a circling surround.

The bedding critters sprang to their feet. Every animal watched him intently, but he never closed the distance, which did not exactly reassure them, but he was too far off for them to start running, so they watched him without moving, prepared to run if he came closer.

He finished the surround and eased up atop the westerly landswell where he'd be in sight when Bud found him, swung off and sat on the ground in front of his horse, tipped down his hat against sunsmash, and made a smoke. They were good cattle. Maybe Bill Burton didn't cull his bulls close, but there was not a gummer cow down there. A few looked to be maybe eight or nine years old and they were all in good flesh. The calves on the ground were already slick as moles with two and three double chins; the cows were making plenty of rich milk. Of course this time of year they'd be doing that anyway, with grass to their hocks, but a rangeman always looked for unthrifty cows anyway.

Bud loped up the landswell from the north, swung off and stood with his reins and romal draped from one arm as he studied the cattle. "See any trouble?" he asked, without looking at Paul.

"No. Some are mighty close though. Maybe a week or so off."

Bud did not suggest making another surrounding ride. He squatted with pleasant morning sun across his shoulders and said, "Tell you what, Paul. You take over watchin' 'em for the next few days." He finally turned toward the youth. "Did you ever pull a hung-up calf?"

"Yes. I guess I've pulled my share of them."

Bud stood up and turned to ease reins over his horse's head. "Good. I'll tell Bill I set you to mindin' this bunch. Now we can head back."

As Paul snugged up his cincha he said. "It's still pretty early, Bud."

The tophand nodded. "Yeah, I know. But I want to talk to Bill, and there's chores around the yard you can do until supper-time."

Three

Bill's Decision

They did not reach the ranch-yard until the sun was slanting away, and when they turned their horses out Bud made a vague gesture. "You might fill the bunkhouse woodbox if you're a mind to." Then he walked away, and Paul stood wearing a faintly puzzled frown.

There had been a sweaty-backed big bay colt in the back corral then they had turned their animals in, and that was reassuring to Bud Fisk. He went through the bunkhouse and rattled the rangeboss's door until Bill called for him to enter.

They exchanged a nod, and Bud headed for a rickety chair, as he hauled off his hat, and said, "Well, what did you find out in town?"

Bill was slow to reply. "I got that dodger off the post office wall, and I talked to George Kimball."

"You told him the kid was out here?"

A flicker of testy annoyance flashed from Burton's gaze. "Of course I didn't. I just bought the sheriff a drink and got him talked around to that poster. He said he had another one at his office, an' he said he had a letter from some lawman over in Nebraska saying there was a five hundred dollar reward out." Bill went to a chair and sat down, shoved out his legs and regarded scuffed boot-toes. "The letter said there was three fellers on the trail."

Bud sat listening and relaxed. He said nothing.

Bill scowled at his boot-toes. "Well, it was some kind of land feud as near as Sheriff Kimball can figure it out." Bill raised his head. "There was a fight. I guess it come closer to bein' a real battle. Afterwards, the kid rode away."

"That's all?" asked Bud Fisk.

"It's all George knew. It's all he said, and he wasn't real interested; they're goin' to have an election in Ridgefield next week. He's worryin' about that more than anything else."

Bud arose and crossed to the bucket with the dipper in it, ladled up a drink of water and returned to his chair. "I saw somethin' today you might be interested in," he said, as he sat down. "I didn't go look for those heifers straight off; just for the pure hell of it I sort of angled around through the foothills watchin' Paul."

"Did he find the bull?"

"Yeah. And we threw it and doctored it. But that's not what I saw, Bill. There was four wolves tryin' to hamstring the old bull. Paul left his horse among some jack-pines, walked down there, stepped out where they could see him —

an' I never in my life seen shootin' like that. He killed three of those wolves before they could run. He drew and got off all three shots faster'n you or me could even draw a gun. Then he killed the last wolf."

Burton sat gazing at his tophand in long silence. Eventually he said, "You want a drink?"

Bud declined. "No. It's too early. What I'm sayin' is that at eighteen years of age he's the fastest man I ever seen with a belt-gun."

"I heard you. I understood what you were saying."

Bill rummaged a shelf for his bottle, and with his back to Bud Fisk mixed water into the glass, then went back to his chair, and, as though the tophand had not mentioned guns, he said, "How did he handle himself around the bull?"

"Fine. I'd guess he's maybe the best young rider I've ever worked with. Someone sure taught him well. I took him to the cottonwood spring and he looked over the heifers. I told him he could keep an eye on 'em for the next few days. I wanted him out where we'd know where he'd be, and away from the yard and the other riders."

Bill sipped lukewarm watered whisky.

Bud waited a long time before impatiently saying, "Well?"

"Well what?"

"Well, gawdammit, what are you goin' to do, Bill?"

The rangeboss sipped more whisky before

replying. "I don't know."

Bud sat studying the other man. He had never before seen the rangeboss unable to reach a decision, and it shocked him. But he wisely said nothing.

"Bud, I don't like the idea of three fellers being on his trail."

"He's got a head-start, Bill. He had one when he rode in here."

"Yeah, that's exactly what I was thinkin' about on the ride back from Ridgefield. He's been here goin' on his second week. Dependin' on how far back those three fellers was, he's lost most of his lead, and maybe all of it. He can ride out of the yard tomorrow, and ride right down three gun-barrels without a chance in hell."

Bud shifted on the chair, then arose with a bitter-eyed look and went over to also pour whisky into a glass half full of water. He turned and bluntly said, "Bill, where is the poster?"

Burton jerked a thumb. "Yonder, on the table under my hat."

Fisk got the dodger, studied the likeness of Paul Franklyn on it, read and reread the printing, tossed the dodger down and went back to his chair with the whisky-glass in his hand.

"We can take him into town tonight. George Kimball can lock him up. When those three fellers arrive in Ridgefield, George can run 'em off or lock them up too."

Bill put aside his emptied glass. "What I'd like

to know, is what actually happened back in Nebraska."

Bud was exasperated. "That dodger says murder. A lawman signed it, so he also signed the murder-warrant, didn't he? Bill — I know about what you're thinkin', but for gosh sakes get rid of this feller. I'll tell you for a fact that no one eighteen years is as good with a gun as Paul is, unless he's worked at it since he was maybe fifteen years old. I'll tell you something else, and you know this as well as I do, no feller who has spent all his spare time learning how to be a gunman suddenly hangs it up and forgets how to shoot people he don't like or gets into an argument with."

Bud suddenly stopped speaking. He remembered the things Paul had said about the lame bull. Back when they had been sitting their horses out there, Bud had tried to square that sympathy for the bull with what he had already known — that Paul Franklyn was a fugitive with a murder charge against him. That bothered him now, so he drained his glass and sat back in the chair gazing at the far wall where Bill Burton's bunk was bolted. Finally, he said, "Well hell, it's up to you."

The rangeboss nodded slowly. "Yeah. Suppose we just keep him out there with the heifers until we can find out what this is all about?"

Bud considered the glass in his work-scarred big hand, and grumbled when he replied. "Weatherford's a cow outfit, not no orphanage.

31

All right; like I said, I had that in mind when I set him to mindin' those heifers. And that reminds me, why didn't he switch horses and use some other name, an' why did he leave a trail they could follow?"

Bill Burton arose and reached for his hat. "I thought about those things on the ride back too. He's pretty young to know how to lose a trail, Bud."

"The hell he is," grumbled Fisk, also arising. "I watched him track that bull today. He can read a sign better'n you or I can."

Bill turned in the doorway. "Then don't it strike you odd how he's acted?"

They walked through the bunkhouse to the sunbright yard before Bud answered. "I was goin' to suggest that maybe he's dumb — but he ain't. I've ridden with him enough to know better'n that."

Bill tugged his hat forward as he ranged a glance around the big, empty yard. "You see? That's what's been goin' through my head — along with one other thing, Bud."

"What other thing?"

"He's not dumb, is he?"

"No."

"Then tell me why he rode in here, and hired on, when he knew there were three men after him — and stayed on?"

Bud saw the cook slip around from the north side of the cookshack to enter his building, and said, "That old bastard's got whiskey hid all over the place." Then he walked off.

Bill felt in a shirt pocket for his plug, bit off a cud and worked it up into his cheek, repocketed the plug and headed for the corrals out back. There was something he particularly wanted to do; on the ride back from town he had worked out what he thought would be the best way to do it. He knew the best way *not* to do it, because asking direct, personal questions was simply not done. It not only would not get an answer back, but it would certainly get Bill cussed out as well.

The riding crew drifted in one at a time. One of them, a lanky Montanan named Walt Poole, bypassed the barn tie-rack and swung off over in front of Bill Burton. Walt was a shrewd, leathery-skinned, laconic man beginning to grey a little above the ears. He turned to tug the latigo loose as he dryly said, "I come by that spring where the cottonwoods grow and saw a couple of those late heifers standing around looking uncomfortable and switchin' their tails. Maybe someone ought to go up there tomorrow."

Bill nodded. "Yeah. Paul's goin' to keep an eye on them for the next few days. Was there any new calves on the ground?"

"No — but I saw some fresh wolf-sign not very far from there."

Bill let the lanky Montanan lead his horse toward the barn without comment. He was thinking of what Bud Fisk had told him about the wolves trying to bait the lame bull. Maybe having Paul Franklyn up there would be more of an advantage than he had thought it might

He did not see the new hand until the *cosinero* beat his triangle summoning everyone to supper, and then he only saw Paul entering the building with two other riders, so he had no opportunity to speak to him privately until later, when it was turning dark and the men trooped to the bunkhouse to set up their nightly poker sessions, and Paul went out to the corrals for his after-supper smoke.

Bud Fisk was the last man to enter the bunkhouse. He watched the rangeboss stroll down the south side of the log barn toward the corrals. He had seen Paul walk back there earlier. Bud sighed and went indoors to join the poker game.

It was another bland late evening, but tonight there was a moon. Not much of a one, and it was tipped downwards, which meant there was rain on the way; at least that was what the Indians believed, and rangeriders adopted the idea and most of them swore by it.

Paul was leaning on the peeled pole stringers building his smoke when Bill Burton walked up. Paul nodded and leaned to strike a match and light up. Bill squinted in at the hay-eating horses and said, "That big bay colt of mine picked up a stone bruise today. I was wonderin' if he was limping."

Paul turned to also look for the bay colt among the other animals. He found it, pitched in a pebble to make the colt move, then removed his cigarette to speak. "Looks sound to me."

34

Bill nodded his head. "Yeah, he looks all right. I was figurin' on ridin' him tomorrow. You and I'll go up there and see how the three-legged bull is getting along. Then we'll swing around and go look at the heifers."

Paul trickled smoke. "Bud told me to mind the heifers for a few days."

Bill knew this. "Yeah. Good idea. Incidentally, when I'm not around, Bud is ramrod."

Paul turned toward the shorter and older man. "The cattle look mighty good."

This was a subject which lay close to the rangeboss's heart. "We do our damnedest to keep 'em that way. Weatherford's got enough range, but we rotate 'em, keep them from eatin' everything down to dust. We could run maybe another couple thousand head, but this way, if we get an early winter or a bad one, there'll be grass for 'em to pay down to. You like the range business, Paul?"

"Yes. Back home we had cattle. Not very many. We were going to build up — keep the best heifers and buy different bulls every couple of years."

Remembering what Bud Fisk had said about the younger man's handiness, the rangeboss asked a question. "Your paw was a stockman, then?"

"Well, no. Back in Missouri where he grew up they farmed, but when we moved to Nebraska he wanted to build up a herd so he could quit farming." Paul dropped the quirley and ground

35

it underfoot. "We'd have got there. My paw was a tophand. He could rope with the best of them. He'd take me out with him to the cattle. I was pretty young, but we worked as a team. He never got mad. I didn't learn very fast, but I learned — and he never got mad."

Paul stopped speaking and ranged a slow look back among the milling horses. The rangeboss settled against the corral, also looking in.

"There are worse things than the cattle business, Paul. A feller your age who can do the work might someday end up being an owner."

The younger man turned slowly to gaze at wiry, leathery Bill Burton. "Someday," he said quietly. "Maybe. Good night."

Burton watched the supple youth head for the bunkhouse. He wore his sixgun low, but most rangemen did. One thing Paul did that most rangeriders did not do; he never rode out without his sixgun, even when all they were going to do was hunt cattle, or make a gather to move the cattle.

The other riders had probably noticed this, but as far as the rangeboss knew no one had said anything about it. Bill turned back to watching the horses. By now they had eaten most of the feed which had been forked over the corral to them, and now the cranky ones were baring their teeth, putting their ears back and making little short runs at the less belligerent horses to have a chance to lip up the few remaining grass stalks.

36

Bill's big bay colt was not one of the belligerent horses. Young horses rarely were, but all the same it annoyed Bill to watch horses half the heft of his bay send the big colt fleeing.

He finally shook his head and headed for the bunkhouse. Across the yard the cookshack was still lighted, but elsewhere around the yard it was dark. Only the bunkhouse showed lights on the west side of the yard. When Bill got closer he could hear someone swearing in there, in a despairing way, which meant one of the crew had just lost a pot he had expected to win.

Four
The Canyon

They headed across open country riding north-westerly in the direction of the foothills with a high mist hanging overhead which did not brighten very much even after sunrise. The rangeboss said it looked as though it might rain, but not for a long while yet, and Paul nodded without comment because he was looking for the lame bull, and thought he saw it near a willow-brake when he pointed.

It was the old bull for a fact. He was lying among some spindly willow-trees chewing his cud. He had been watching the horsemen for an hour. By the time they got close enough to see him too, the bull was accustomed to their presence and did not make an effort to arise. They halted back a short distance so that the rangeboss could make his judgement.

A pair of furtive coyotes skulked among the willows in an effort to surreptitiously put distance between themselves and the rangemen. They knew better than to bust out and run for it. Two shots would be all it would take, and no critter on earth could outrun a bullet.

Paul saw that grey, faint movement, turned, made out the coyotes, watched them briefly then turned back toward the bull without saying a word.

Bill Burton pouched a chew into his cheek, and spat once. Then he said, "Let's get him up. I'd like to see how much swellin' he's got. What was it, a splinter?"

"Snake-bite."

They eased ahead until the bull blew out a big, wet snort and made a ponderous wag of his horns at them. Bill grinned. Like all rangemen he understood critters. They walked their horses another couple of yards, passed the invisible line which the bull had fixed in his mind as his limit of safety, and the bull heaved three times before he got all that bulk upright. To Paul's surprise he was putting weight on the injured foot. There was still swelling, and a little caked blood, but nowhere nearly as much heat and swelling as there had been.

Burton drew rein. The men and horses returned the bull's unblinking regard. He had by now pretty well figured out that they were not going to rope him or make him move. He did not menace them with his horns, but neither did he bring up another cud.

Bill finally sat back in the saddle. "Tucked up, but not too bad off."

Paul agreed, and they left the bull at his bed as they rode in the opposite direction deeper into the foothills. Bill said nothing until they had covered more than a mile, then without explaining he abruptly altered course, riding directly toward that little hidden canyon where his graves were. Nor did he say anything until they passed beyond the shouldering hills which formed the canyon's mouth and had the cemented red-stone cross in sight, and the two graves. Then he tugged off his gloves, shoved them under his belt, halted back a short way from the graves and said, "I pull weeds up here once in a while. Care to lend a hand?"

The horses were hobbled. Paul was uncomfortable and he was silent. They pulled weeds, leaving just the budding flowers, until the graves looked presentable again, then Bill cocked an eye at the sun, which was just now beginning to brighten the little secret place, and said, "I guess there's not many things worse than bein' alone." He turned slowly toward the taller, younger man. "A man needs something. But a family don't have to be kinfolk, does it? It's better that way, but then we got no control over most things." He paused, sought a place to sit, then hunkered down as the warming sun reached in to winnow away nightlong cold. "When I was your age my folks hitched up to drive to town for supplies. They never come back. I was fifteen then."

Paul sat down slowly and tipped his hat to avoid sunlight. "What happened?"

"In'ians. That was across the Missouri oppo-

40

site Council Bluffs. When I was a kid we used to watch our folks. If they stood still and listened, we knew what it might be, and many's the time I could hear my heart beatin' as loud as a grouse thumpin' on a log." Bill picked up a twig, pulled out his Barlow knife and whittled.

Paul said, "Did you go after the In'ians?"

"I didn't. I had a sister to look after. She was nine. And there was wood to be cut and animals to be minded. The army went after 'em. They was Omahas, supposed to be friendly and all. The army settled up with 'em. It wasn't just my folks they killed."

Paul pulled a grass stalk and chewed it in silence for a while before speaking. "I'll tell you something, Bill. I'd like to stay. Weatherford's a good place. The riders are nice fellers, the grub is good. You 'n Bud been real decent to me. But I better ride on. I should have rode on a week ago; it was just that it was real nice here. Like you said, a man needs something."

Bill shoved back his hat, then continued whittling. "It's too late," he said quietly.

Paul turned quickly and stared.

Bill flung the stick away. "Boy, whatever happened back there, you got three riders on your back-trail."

Paul continued to stare. The shock of discovering that the man beside him *knew*, held him silent.

"Listen to me, Paul; I've lived a long time. I've learned some of the rules of livin', and one of

41

them is that you can't outrun things. I don't give a damn how far you go, nor how fast, you can't get clear of things."

Finally, the younger man said, "How did you find out?"

"Well, for one thing there's a dodger out on you."

"This far away?"

"Yes. I brought one back from town with me yesterday. George Kimball, the sheriff at Ridgefield, has another one. He told me they wanted you for murder as the result of some sort of land feud, or something."

Paul slumped slowly. "I was better'n thirty days on the trail, seventeen days of it crossin' this high ridge range country. How the hell did they get that information this far away, so quick?"

Bill shrugged. "Telegraph, maybe. Or maybe just by mail. While you was runnin' they was posting those damned dodgers. Anyway, that's not the trouble."

"Bill, I got to go."

"Paul, I just told you — it's too late. Did you know there were three men on your back-trail?"

"I kept watch; I guess I knew, but I thought I'd lost them a couple of weeks back."

"Who are they?"

"My cousins, my uncle's three boys. Harry, Rob and Joe."

Bill showed surprise. "Your cousins?"

"I guess if you know half of it you'd ought to

know all of it, Bill. My paw wanted to grow his herd of cattle. The land was there, no one owned it unless maybe it had belonged to the In'ians, but they'd been chased away. So paw brushed it out with his big team and we ranged some of it, but my maw's brother, Uncle Gus, he wanted to run cattle out there too, an' told my paw he'd figured to use it first."

"An' they had an argument?"

Paul nodded. "My maw went over to talk with Uncle Gus. He run her off. My paw didn't take kindly to that. He drove the cattle onto the brushed-off country, and took to wearin' a gun. He met Uncle Gus and his boys. All I ever knew about what happened was that the boys brought paw home in a wagon — dead. He'd been hit six times. My maw went into a sort of fit. I buried paw close to the cabin. One night my maw hitched the team to the wagon and drove over to Uncle Gus's place. I didn't even know she'd gone until morning when I looked out and seen her sittin' on the wagon-seat in the cold, the horses standing in their harness with their noses against the shed. I guess they'd brought her home some time before daylight."

Paul turned aside, spat, and turned back only as far as the graves. He sat looking at them without speaking.

"They swore they didn't hurt her, that she and Uncle Gus had a hell of a row, and he run her off. She had a broken collar-bone and some busted ribs. A neighbour-lady come to care for her, but

43

I guess it was like she said, maw didn't want to live — an' she was sort of crazy most of the time. Then she died and I buried her beside paw. Well, the neighbour-lady took my sister home with her. I said I'd stay on the place and mind things."

"But you didn't."

"Yes. I did for a while, but every time I'd lug a pail past the graves — Well, paw and I used to practice with guns a lot. You had to when you lived out like we did. I practiced by myself with his gun-belt, but I was already pretty good. He used to say it was a bad thing for a feller to be so well co-ordinated he could draw and kill as good as I could. I saddled up one night after leavin' a note on the kitchen table for my sister, and rode over to Uncle Gus's place. Harry, Joe and Rob were campin' out with the cattle."

"Where was his wife?"

"He didn't have one. She died before I was born, tryin' to birth Joe — he's the youngest. There was a full moon. I reined up out front and called Uncle Gus. When he stepped outside I told him to get his pistol. He stood there lookin' at me like he thought I was crazy, then he reached along the wall and stepped out onto the porch with a shotgun in his hands. He cut loose before I had any idea he was goin' to do it — and killed the horse I was riding. Then he run at me with the other barrel cocked — and I shot him twice. He never got off that second blast, which was just as well because he wasn't more'n fifteen

44

feet from me. I couldn't have ducked anyway, the horse was layin' atop my right leg. I hit him in the brisket both times. He was dead before he hit the ground. I took one of their horses, put my outfit on him, got astride and started riding — that's all of it."

"How was the leg?"

"It hurt for a couple weeks, then stopped hurting."

Paul did not meet Bill's gaze. He spat out the grass stalk and ranged a slow look over at the larger grave and the smaller one. "It wasn't murder, Bill. You can't hardly murder a man who has shot at you with a scattergun, can you?"

"There's a warrant on you, boy, an' a five hundred dollar bounty."

Paul made a death's-head grin. "Yeah. Well — the feller who made out that paper — my maw had three brothers, Uncle Gus, the one I shot, Uncle Abe, who went out to California before I was born an' never came back — and Uncle John Moore. He was the sheriff of our county. He'd sign the paper against me, and most likely he put up the bounty too. He's well set-up back there; owns farmland, racehorses, a nice log house."

Bill Burton jettisoned his cud and glanced again in the direction of the graves, then he sat so long in thoughtful, deep silence that when something snapping a twig south of the horses, midway back down to the opening into the little canyon, caught Paul's attention, Bill only half-heard it.

Paul was moving, gathering himself to jump up, when Bill looked southward, and reached with surprising speed to grab cloth and hiss an order. "Sit still!"

A dry, deep voice spoke from beyond the shielding horses. "That's good advice, young feller. Just set there and keep your hands in sight. You too, Bill."

The speaker did not show himself for a full minute. When he finally stepped away from the horses he was holding a cocked saddlegun in both hands, low across his belly. He was a large man with curly grey hair, slightly bow-legged, and with arms and legs like oak.

He walked very carefully without once taking his eyes off Paul Franklyn. When he was close enough he gave an order. "Bill, lift out his gun. Go on now, do as I say."

Burton did not obey. He regarded the big man a long while before speaking. "What are you doin' up here, George?"

"Take his gun and pitch it away, Bill!"

Finally, the rangeboss obeyed. When Paul had been disarmed the large man lowered the hammer on his Winchester. "I guess you better shed yours too, Bill. Go on now, *do it!*"

Again the rangeboss obeyed. Then, finally, the large man let his carbine sag, and allowed some of the alert stiffness to leave his body as he studied Paul with frank curiosity before addressing the rangeboss again.

"You'd make a hell of an outlaw, Bill," he

said, strolling closer and grounding his carbine to lean on. "Old Jeff saw you take down that dodger at the post office yesterday. He told me about it. I got to speculating. You asked a lot of questions about this young feller while we were at the saloon. Usually, we talked about the range, the weather, cattle prices. In all the years I've known you, Bill —" Sheriff Kimball wagged his head. "Why in the hell didn't you just *tell* me, or why didn't you bring him in yourself?"

Bill looked at the ground in front. Eventually he said, "How'd you find us up here?"

"Your *cosinero* told me about a hurt bull and what he'd heard at breakfast about you an' him comin' up here to look for the bull. After I got out aways it wasn't hard to track you." The large man turned steady eyes on Paul. "Boy, pull up your pants-legs."

Bill snorted. "He don't carry no hideout-gun, for Chris'sake!"

"Pull 'em up, boy!"

Paul obeyed, the older men looked, then George Kimball waved a hand, and as Paul leaned to lower the pants-legs Sheriff Kimball faced Bill Burton again. "I been out there for a quarter-hour."

"Then you heard what he told me."

Sheriff Kimball's expression did not change. "Yeah, I heard. And I know what you're goin' to say, and I'll give you my answer before you open your mouth. This buckaroo is wanted for murder. How he did it, where he did, don't

47

mean a damned thing to me. There's a legal warrant out on him, and my job is to catch him and lock him up, an' after that it's up to the authorities back where he killed that man. Bill, this isn't the first time I've run into something like this. My job is to fetch him back to town, lock him up, and notify the folks who want him that I got him. There aren't any ifs, ands, or buts. I'll tell you something else — darn you anyway — by rights I'd ought to take you back with me too. You knew who he was, but you didn't tell me a damned thing. That makes you an accessory. Shut up! Don't open your mouth, Bill! Now, you two, get on your feet — stay in front of me, don't move fast and stay so's I can see your hands all the time. Bill, when we get down near the ranch you go on home. I'm not goin' to take you in, but by gawd I'd ought to. Now get up, both of you!"

Five

Heading Back

There was heat beyond the hidden canyon which had not been present back up near the graves, and the horses were thirsty, so Bill Burton led the way over to the cottonwood spring which would have been his ultimate destination before this day had ended, if Sheriff Kimball had not appeared.

The sheriff was tight-lipped for most of the way over to the spring, and his hard, uncompromising gaze fell upon Paul with no hint of mercy, but when it fell upon Bill Burton there was more disapproval than rancour. When they saw the cattle down upon the far side of the westerly landswell and headed for them, there was a quick stir of anxiety among the cows with little calves; they always had a very strong protective instinct when their calves were very young.

Bill studied the cattle as he rode down closer to the spring. It was his lifelong nature to examine every head of livestock he encountered. As the cattle began to yield ahead of the horseman one big heifer hung back, acting as though she wanted very much to follow the others but could not bring herself to do it, and Sheriff Kimball, who had been a rangeman for many years, called to Bill.

"Give her ground. We don't have to go over there anyway."

They went far out and around the heifer, reached the water-hole and swung off to loosen latigos and remove bridles. As the horses dropped their heads to drink Bill turned to gaze back as he said, "She's got a calf hidden in the brush over there sure as hell."

Kimball nodded, leaned across his saddle also gazing back, and when Paul said, "It'll be a dead one," the big lawman scowled at him.

Bill stared back there without speaking for a long while, then he said, "I'm going to look, George."

Kimball did not dissent; the rangeboss was not in custody, he probably should have been, but he wasn't. Nevertheless Sheriff Kimball watched darkly as Bill walked his horse in the direction of the agitated big heifer.

When he was close enough he could see the milk squirting from all four quarters. He tried to get behind the big heifer to ascertain whether she actually had had a calf, but she would not allow that; she kept turning with Bill, facing him every moment, so he gave that up and rode around through some low scrub brush and tall grass, then halted stonestill and sat a long time without moving. Finally, he reined around and started walking his horse back.

Paul and George Kimball could see his face before he got up to them. The sheriff, whose horse had raised its head from the waterhole, said, "Dead?"

Bill nodded and swung off to lead his animal back to the spring. "Yeah. Wolves." Bill was angry. "I've never used poison but I'm thinkin' of using it right now."

Paul spoke up. "Did you ever see one die from poisoning, Bill? It'd make you sick to watch that."

George Kimball swung slowly to regard his prisoner. Eventually he motioned for his companions to mount up, and set the example. As they were riding clear of the spring, cattle which were out aways began to warily return to their water-hole.

They started angling southernward so as to break out of the foothills a mile closer to the homeplace. For as long as the broken country inhibited it, they rode in single file with Kimball in the rear, but when they were closer to the end of the rough country, had open range in sight ahead, Kimball eased up beside Paul Franklyn and said, "Why the hell didn't you ride right on through, boy?"

Paul gazed at the big man's heavy features for a moment before replying. "Because I didn't have any money, an' because my horse was leg-weary, an' because I just wanted to stop somewhere — find a place to be with people for a little while."

"They'd have caught you, boy."

Paul turned to gaze ahead where the hills were peeling back to expose miles of grassland. He did not say a word, but Bill did. He twisted in the saddle to scowl at Sheriff Kimball. "His uncle's the feller who signed the warrant, an' he's the head lawman back there, George. Even if his cousins don't kill him before he gets back there, what kind of a trial will he get?"

"Fair one as far as I know, Bill, and as far as you know too. I've never been in a country where *everyone* takes one side."

The rangeboss snorted and straightened around in the saddle. Sheriff Kimball was not finished though. "I didn't like his story any better than you did, Bill, but I've heard men in his position lie like hell. For all I know that's what he did with you back there — lied like hell."

Paul turned slowly toward Sheriff Kimball. "I didn't lie. Why should I lie? Back there, I was talkin' to a man who's been real decent to me — and I didn't know a lawman was within fifty miles of me. Why would I have lied, Sheriff?"

Kimball spat before replying. "I got no idea, boy, except that I can tell you from personal knowledge that most outlaws will lie when the truth would fit better. Now I'm tired of talkin' about all this."

They had twin low mounds dead ahead, one on each side of them but a fair distance from the centre of the flat country they were traversing. The heat came up this far into the foothills to meet them, and out across open country it was lying in faint waves. It probably did not help any that the thin, veil-like overcast Bill had commented upon after sunrise was still up there, a great diaphanous veil of it which did not obscure the sun, but rather diffused its light, and added to both heat and humidity. The horses had felt this more than their riders had, which was why they had been thirsty back yonder.

They had seen nothing but scrub and a few trees, and the little, low, sometimes fat, sometimes lean, upended foothills they had been riding through since leaving the cottonwood spring. The open country offered an immense vista of monotonous sameness interspersed distantly and at infrequent intervals by little stands of trees. This time of day that was where rangemen looked first for cattle, in those cool, shady places.

George Kimball attempted a lighter conversation when he said, "Bill, it's a good grass year."

The rangeboss nodded without looking around or speaking.

Kimball tried again. "The Weatherfords will make money this year; good grass, plenty of it, good water and all."

"They'll always make money off the ranch," retorted Bill Burton, "if I got anything to say about it."

Kimball was piqued. "There's somebody else

53

who's got more to say about it than you." Kimball jerked a gloved thumb upwards.

Bill snapped an answer back. "Yeah. Well, Him and I've been workin' together for a long time. We don't have to sell our souls to make a living!"

Kimball's face got splotchy red and he closed his mouth, hard. They were riding into the wide slot between those two fat low-mounded foothills. He ranged a sparking-mad glance ahead and to both sides, and abruptly hauled back on his reins while letting go a sudden loud breath. "Hold it," he snapped. "Bill, rein up!"

That was all Sheriff Kimball had time to say, and both his surprised companions were looking around and slackening pace when the first gunshot sounded flat, hard and vicious. They did not see the gunman, and probably because of the distance their horses did not shy at the muzzle-blast, but when all three men dropped from the saddle the horses finally fidgeted.

Kimball gave a sharp order. "Get back. Get the hell back out of here. He's atop that low hill to our right, an' he's using a Winchester."

The second carbine shot came from closer and upon the opposite side of the flat place, and this time the gunman scored. Paul Franklyn went down in a flung-back, sprawling heap. Bill dropped his reins and ran over to grab cloth and try to lift the younger man. Paul's breath was bursting out in gasps because of pain, and he remained doubled over until Sheriff Kimball appeared, grabbed with both hands and flung the younger man across his powerful shoulder as though he were nothing more than a sack of wheat. With his carbine in his free hand Kimball said, "Bill — your damned bay horse ran off. Get the other two and get back out of here. *Move, damn it!*"

Kimball lumbered northward in a bear-like lope, with blood from the man on his shoulder trickling down his shirt-front. Bill caught the remaining two horses and ran between them in Kimball's wake. Sweat poured out of him. Up ahead, the big sheriff was pumping for breath but did not slow down until he was beyond carbine range, then he turned like a bear at bay, still clutching his carbine, and glared defiantly back.

The third gunshot sounded. Kimball winced, then attempted to whirl, and staggered under his burden. Behind him Bill Burton called out. "I saw the smoke. The son of a bitch is on the left and behind us. George, they got us in the middle. Head for those jack-pines."

The distance would not normally have been difficult to handle, but Sheriff Kimball, although a large, powerful man, was carrying a man nearly as tall as he was, if not as broad, and the ground sloped uphill. He sounded like a wind-broke horse by the time he had reached the first three or four spindly pines, and sagged to his knees to rid himself of Paul Franklyn.

Burton got the horses into the timber, hurriedly tethered them, and went back down to help Kimball carry the younger man deeper into shade and shelter. Then Bill straightened up and glared. "What did you do with those guns you took off us back yonder?"

Between great gulps of air Sheriff Kimball answered just as furiously. "I left 'em up there. What'd you expect me to do with 'em!"

"Fetch 'em along, you damned fool. You got one sixgun an' one carbine. There are three of those men out there!"

Kimball suddenly flung his carbine. "Take it. Now you'd ought to feel better." As he finished speaking he looked down, then up again. "Keep watch. They got to have at us from both sides and in front." He knelt beside Paul, dropped his riding-gloves in the pine needles and opened the younger man's blood slippery shirt. When he glanced up Bill was still standing there, his face twisted as he looked at the wounded man. Sheriff Kimball rocked back, and with both big hands upon his legs very quietly said, "Bill, maybe you're the best stockman in the country, but you aren't worth a damn in a fight like this one." He paused, then raised his voice in suppressed fury. *"Gawddamn you, go back down there and watch for them!"*

Bill stepped past and continued to walk until he was in view of the silent, empty, sunbright country on both sides and dead ahead. There was nothing out there, not even any high-circling buzzards.

He was thirsty, wet with sweat, and badly

upset. Whether Sheriff Kimball thought so or not, Bill Burton had indeed been in fights like this before, but it had been a long time ago.

Right now, he had churning insides. He dug out his plug, gnawed off a corner, checked the cud, spat once, and immediately began to feel better. Once, he turned to glance back, but he could see little except George Kimball's broad back, so he stepped a little closer to the first tier of timber and knelt on one knee beside a rough-barked young red fir-tree.

Behind them, the slope got fairly steep and it was open all the way to the top, a distance of perhaps three hundred yards. Indians would have charged down that hillside, howling and brandishing weapons, but no white man in his right mind would do anything like that, and Sheriff Kimball could see out through the rearward trees.

Out front, where Bill Burton masticated and knelt watching, the grass was nearly stirrup-high, and there was chaparral nearly man-high to the right, northward, but between the chaparral clump and the trees where Bill was kneeling was only tall grass, and the sun was close enough to being directly overhead to show every grass-head; if they attempted to crawl toward the trees from the chaparral clump the grass-heads would move. Bill liked the idea of them trying that, but although he was still watching fifteen minutes later when big George Kimball came glumly along and squatted nearby, not a single one of those tall, wand-like grass-heads moved.

Kimball mopped off sweat with a soiled cuff, reset his hat and looked out and around as he said, "I guess we got some idea who those sons of bitches are."

Bill shifted his cud before answering. "Yeah. Since when don't lawmen fetch along the weapons they take off people?"

Kimball make an almost mournful sigh, still looking ahead and on both sides. "To tell you the truth, Bill, I didn't once take my eyes off Franklyn. The damned guns didn't mean anything to me." Then Kimball turned to face the rangeboss. "Did you know this was going to happen? Well, neither did I. Now shut up about those guns, will you? Have you seen anything out there?"

"Nothing," replied the irritated rangeboss, "and maybe I ain't worth a damn in a fight like this, but I know enough not to come down here like you did, and leave the back slope unwatched."

Kimball heaved back up to his full height as though to turn back. "I came down here to tell you that your cowboy got a hell of a gouge alongside his ribs on the left side, an' bled like a stuck hog."

"Bad, George?"

Kimball twisted to glance back through the trees as he answered. "No. It looks like hell though. I got the bleedin' stopped using his shirt to do it. The doctor in town could cut the ragged hide and sew it up, and he'll be fine in a few weeks. No busted ribs. That's what I was worried about."

Bill stood up. "The doctor in town." He spat. "We got two weapons to their maybe six weapons. We're two men against three — the doctor in town my butt!"

Sheriff Kimball turned on his heel and strode furiously back through the trees to keep watch along that rearward slope. In all the years he had known Bill Burton, he had never suspected Bill could be so damned irritable.

Six

The Reaction

That was the end of it; three gunshots from hiding, Paul Franklyn wounded, Bill's bay colt loose somewhere on the range, perhaps heading home, and neither a sighting nor a sound for two hours.

Sheriff Kimball finally said, "I'll ride out. I think they left after they saw your cowboy go down. That's what they been trying to do ever since they commenced following him."

Bill Burton nodded his head. He too did not believe the bushwhackers were still out there. "Be careful," he told the sheriff, and watched Kimball go back, untie his horse, snug up, then mount and rein forward. As he passed the place where Bill was leaning, he said, "I don't think I'd better take him all the way to town, Bill. Not in his shape." Then Kimball ducked under some low limbs and walked his horse out into afternoon sunshine, his sixgun in his lap, his head swinging from side to side like an old boar bear.

Nothing happened. No one shot at him, no one sang out, and no one stood up to show him-

60

self. Bill went back where Paul was lying, knelt to lean on the sheriff's carbine and studied the ashen face of the younger man. "Close," he said. "Whoever he was, he's a pretty good shot. That was long-range shooting. How do you feel?"

Paul looked steadily upwards from pain-glazed eyes. "Where are they?"

"Gone. The sheriff's out there lookin' around. We're goin' to have trouble gettin' you back down out of here. He wrapped you pretty good, but ridin' a horse will likely start the bleedin' again."

"Did you see any of them, Bill?"

"No. But they knew where we were. I've been wonderin' how they knew that. Anyway, there was one on each side, and one farther back. I think the only thing that saved all of us is that they saw you go down." Bill blew out a ragged breath. "I guess George or me had better go to the ranch for a wagon."

Except for Bill's loose horse they might have had to do that. As it turned out, two riders were in the yard when the colt came in dripping sweat and riderless. Those two men immediately hitched a light wagon to a snorty team and back-tracked expecting to find the rangeboss with a broken leg or maybe a cracked spine.

George Kimball heard them coming, scouted them up, then rode up a hillside to wig-wag with his hat. When they reached the little spit of pines both rangemen were big-eyed.

Bill explained what had happened as they were

placing Paul upon the bed of the old wagon. Sheriff Kimball sat his horse watching from a glum face, and when the wagon started away and Bill brought Paul's saddle-horse out of the trees Kimball held out a big paw.

"I'd like to borrow your plug," he said.

Bill handed it over. When he got it back he too bit off a cud, then they started down-country in the wake of the wagon as he said, "They're settin' back yonder somewhere, watching."

Kimball spat aside. "I got an idea, Bill. We're goin' to bury your cowboy." Kimball spat again, he evidently was not an accomplished tobacco chewer. "They don't know whether they killed him or not. The way he went down it looked to me like he wasn't never goin' to get up again, and I was a lot closer than they were. We'll have a burial at the Weatherford place; dig a hole and wrap something big in canvas, and plant it."

Bill thought this over for a hundred yards before speaking. "It'll get them off his trail. But you're still goin' to haul him in on that warrant, aren't you? What good will it do to pretend he was killed and we buried him?"

Kimball spat again and grimaced. "What kind of plug is this? Burns my throat worse than brandy."

"Muleshoe, and it's good quality tobacco. You just aren't a chewer, George."

Kimball spat out his cud, coughed several times, then said, "He's going to be flat on his back in your bunkhouse, and you're going to

62

make sure he stays that way. Put someone to settin' in there with him. Then you have the hole dug and make the bundle and go through the whole ceremony of planting him. Me, I'm goin' to get up a posse and skulk far back and watch. I got a feelin' they won't leave the country until they're plumb certain your cowboy is dead — and buried. If I find three strangers out there spyin' on the ranch, I'll catch them."

Bill Burton was a more direct man. "Sounds complicated to me. Suppose they're high-tailing it right now; we'll be going through all this hocus-pocus and they'll be two hundred miles away and still riding. I think you'd do better to make up your posse right now, today, and hunt up their sign and run them down."

Kimball squinted at the distant sight of rooftops when he replied. "I figure to do that, too, the minute I get back to town. I'm just telling you what your part will be in this damned mess."

Bill thought that over too, and liked it better, so eventually he nodded.

They were within sight of the yard, dusk was not far off, two men were standing like statues looking out where the wagon was bumping along, and Bill jettisoned his cud to make a request.

"Send the doctor out when you get back to town."

Sheriff Kimball nodded. "After dark. You wouldn't need a doctor for a dead man."

Bill snorted, but said nothing.

When they entered the yard even the fat *cosinero* was over at the barn, faintly aromatic from whiskey-breath, but not only willing to help carry Paul to the bunkhouse, but to also go after the doctoring kit he kept in the cookshack. He was older than anyone on the place excepting Bill Burton, had been a rangeman all his life, and had over the years become very adept at patching things like broken bones and gunshot wounds.

The riders remained inside with Paul and the cook. Bill went down to the horse-barn to care for the animals, and found that Bud Fisk had already parked the light wagon, hauled off the harness, draped it from its wooden pegs, and was starting to care for Paul's horse.

Bud said, "Well — so the sons of bitches caught up to him, eh?"

Bill nodded. "I'd like to know how they knew where he was — up in the foothills with me."

Bud had a valid answer to that. "Easy. They just lay out there somewhere, maybe since last night, and watched. When you and him rode off they followed you. Bill, they had all the advantage. Hell, we didn't even know they were in the country."

The rangeboss accepted this, not just because it was plausible but also because it was more a matter of curiosity with him than it was of genuine interest.

He took his outfit from Bud and went to the pole to fling it up there. Then he said, "The one that hit him was a damned good shot."

Bud had an answer for that too. "They mostly are, back where those fellers came from. They been shootin' the heads of grey-squirrels for supper since they been little kids. How did George find you?"

Bill fidgeted; that was an embarrassing question. He had thought he was being very sly over in town yesterday, and Kimball had read him like an open book. "Tracked us," he muttered, and changed the subject, explained about the mock funeral, and walked out to the corral with Fisk as the tophand led the horse out to be turned in. They stood a while looking at Bill's bay colt. He was dry now, but there was caked salt-sweat on him from racing for home when he got loose.

Bud rubbed his hooked nose with two fingers, looking dubious, and said, "That don't sound to me like it's goin' to help much. Those boys may not be that gullible."

Bill would have argued that point with anyone. "You weren't there. If you'd seen Paul go down, and how he passed out later when I was tryin' to lift him, you'd think he was bad hit too."

Fisk shrugged. If the rangeboss had his mind made up, that was how things were going to be done. But Bud had a suggestion to offer.

"Kimball's on his way back to town. If you and him got things figured right, those damned bushwhackers will be watching him too."

Bill was fishing for his plug again and did not comment.

"So," stated the tophand, putting a shrewd gaze upon Burton, "what'd be wrong with me and maybe Walt riding out after dusk? Whether you 'n Kimball are right or not, about those boys not leaving the country, one thing is a gut-cinch, Bill, they're going to make a camp somewhere tonight, and we know this country backwards and forwards. You go ahead and make plans for the burial, George can raise a hullabaloo in town, and Walt will ride with me lookin' for those boys in the dark. One or the other of these plans ought to stir up something."

Bill chewed, watched dusk come slowly down from the high country, and leaned on the corral stringers. Eventually he straightened up and grunted. "All right."

Bud looked down. "But you think it'll be a waste of time."

Bill nodded. "Yeah. They're not goin' to make a fire, Bud. Not after tryin' to murder a man. But if you're willin' to lose some sleep it's all right with me."

Fisk shrugged again. "Even if I didn't like the feller they shot, I don't like how they tried to do it."

"I thought you didn't like him. Last night you wanted me to —"

"That had nothing to do with liking Paul, Bill. I *do* like him, but he's still wanted for murder."

The rangeboss sighed and sagged tiredly

66

against the peeled-log stringers. "I need a drink," he said. "Come on over to my room."

They did not make it, the *cosinero* beat on his triangle summoning all hands to supper over at the cookshack.

It was not the customary rowdy time at day's end. There was some talk, mostly bitter, about what had happened, and there was some speculation about why those three men had done it, but since the riders did not know as much about Paul Franklyn as Bud and Bill knew, their supper-table conversation was foot-loose speculation and came nowhere near the actual reason for the bushwhacking.

Later, when everyone was over at the bunkhouse, including the fat, lame cook, Bill patiently explained about the mock funeral, which did not make a whole lot of sense to the rangeriders, so they watched Burton and said almost nothing. Paul was also listening to Bill and watching him. He looked a little better and evidently he felt a little better, but he was as weak as a kitten.

When Bill went through to his private quarters Walt Poole put a shrewd gaze upon the tophand and dryly said, "Bud, I keep feelin' like there's somethin' missin' in all this."

Fisk's answer was curt. "Get your coat. You and I're goin' to ride out a little tonight."

The lanky Montanan did not say a word, he took down his heavy coat from the wooden peg beside his bunk and followed Bud Fisk

67

out into the settling night.

It was warm, there was a high mistiness which probably contributed to this warmth, and it also made the moon and stars seem as though they were under water.

Walt did not say a word until they were rigged out and getting astride out front, then he said, "I lost six bits in the poker game last night and figured to win it back tonight."

They were leaving the yard when Fisk commented on that. "You can loaf six bits' worth the next time you ride out alone. That'll make it up."

The Montanan was silent until they had warmed out their fresh horses, then, settling comfortably against the cantle he asked a question. "They didn't just up and shoot Paul for the hell of it, did they?"

Bud was pulling on his gloves when he answered. "No. They been on his back-trail for maybe a month or more."

"Does he know them?"

"Yeah; he knows them. We're lookin' for the light of a campfire. My guess is that they most likely headed toward town, but well above it, near the foothills."

"Why didn't you tell me this at the bunkhouse. I'd have brought my Winchester."

"You won't need it in the dark, Walt. If we can find their camp we can crawl up on them in the dark."

—The lanky man ranged a look ahead and to

both sides. He was thinking about three bush-whackers now, maybe somewhere up ahead in the darkness. He was no longer speculating about why Paul had been shot, which was exactly why Bud Fisk had changed the subject a half-mile back.

It was not a good night for manhunting. No dark night was for that matter, but that high mistiness partially obscured what little visibility there might otherwise have been, and they had been riding for about two hours, slowly, carefully, mostly silently, when Walt Poole said, "What's the sheriff doing? This is his job."

Fisk had no idea what George Kimball was doing, but he suspected that George was either eating supper at the café in town, about now, or was leaning pleasantly relaxed in front of the bar having a few drinks. "He'll do his job, Walt; we're just maybe doing a little of it for him tonight."

"We're wasting time an' losing sleep is what we're doing, Bud."

He was exactly right, but this had been Bud Fisk's idea, and Bud was in some ways a stubborn man. When the late-night chill arrived, however, and they both shrugged into their coats, even Bud was ready to admit failure.

They had seen no campfire, had sighted no riders, had covered a lot of miles, were cold, tired, and Walt at least was disgusted. He at least had not thought it was a very good idea from the outset.

69

Seven

A Dead Man!

There was not a lot of discussion about the mock funeral, although the men did not appear to think much of Sheriff Kimball's idea even though it was different from what they ordinarily did by daylight, and that perhaps should have cheered them a little.

But they went through all the proper motions, even to dusting their hats and greasing their boots, and manufacturing a believable bundle rolled in old soiled canvas which they placed in the same light wagon Paul had returned to the ranch in the previous day, and rode out to the Weatherford burial-grounds, and started digging.

It was shady out there. The burial-ground lay in a wide, shallow shale with trees around and across it. There were seven graves out there. Bill and Bud Fisk were wearing their go-to-meeting dark coats, and Bill had his Bible sagging in one coat pocket.

The only member of the Weatherford crew not out there was the *cosinero*. He had been left behind at the bunkhouse to look after Paul Franklyn.

When they had the hole dug Bill took them back to the wagon, which was parked in fragrant cottonwood shade, produced a bottle and passed it around.

Bill had never allowed drinking on the ranch, especially during the riding season. Many cow outfits had that rule, but mostly, they were more strict about it than Bill Burton was.

While they all leaned in pleasant shade passing around the bottle, Bud Fisk had been making a close, slow study of the country roundabout. When the bottle came to him he accepted it, held it without drinking from it, and said, "There was a reflection of sunlight off a cheekpiece or a bit." He did not point, but he jutted his jaw Indian-fashion to indicate the north-easterly country.

Walt Poole dryly said, "It won't be the bush-whackers, Bud. You an' I like to froze our chingalees off in that area last night, without seeing a soul."

Bill said, "Kimball, most likely, and his posse-men."

They put aside the bottle, lifted out the straw-filled canvas bundle, and solemnly carried it to the hole and eased it down to the bottom of the grave. As they were doing this Bud Fisk said, "George better be across their trail. When they see us pilin' dirt on their victim they'll turn tail."

Bill Burton was fidgeting a little about this too. He had known Sheriff Kimball a long time, and if George had ever been one of those zealous lawmen it had to have been before Bill Burton knew him. Kimball rarely left town. Yesterday, when he had seen George up in the little hidden canyon it had crossed his mind, but very briefly, that the reason George would try and do something spectacular about now was because of that election he was going to try and win next week.

But Bill said nothing. He planted his hat upon the rim of the near-side rear wagon-wheel, dug out his Bible, said a brief few words over the grave, pocketed the Bible and led the men over for another drink from the bottle. Then they had all struck out for home, and the grizzled, short man who had done most of that digging back yonder had another snort from the bottle on the ride back, then said, "Bill, there wasn't nothin' said about diggin' graves when I hired on."

Burton looked around, considered the older rider, and finally said, "Jess, three times in the past two months I've come onto you sound asleep under a tree when you was supposed to be combin' the foothills for wolves. You want me to pay you for diggin' that grave, or fire you for loafing?"

The men chuckled. Even the aggrieved range-man got a twinkle in his eye.

Bill waited until they were in the yard to announce that there would be no more work for what was left of the day, then he went along to the bunkhouse.

The cook was spinning some long-winded tale

72

of his rangeriding days, complete with arm gestures, and stopped in mid-motion when Bill entered. The rangeboss knew the signs and simply said, "You better go start dinner," then went over beside Paul's bunk; the wounded man was asleep.

Bud and Walt Poole came along a little later to also look in on young Franklyn. Their noise awakened him. Bill was scowling; George Kimball had not sent the doctor out from Ridgefield last night as he had promised to do.

Fisk went over and looked down. "How do you feel?" he asked solicitously.

Paul considered his answer for a while before giving it. "If you mean, compared to a gut-shot bear, or a pole-axed bull, maybe pretty fair."

Bud grinned. "There's a little whiskey out in the wagon."

Paul shook his head. "No thanks. Did you fellers get me buried?"

Before anyone could answer, that grizzled, sinewy rider appeared in the door. "Shooting," he exclaimed. "North-east and quite a few shots."

When the men got out of the bunkhouse, two riders were standing in the middle of the yard looking in the direction of those gunshots. One of them turned as Bill and Bud hastened up. "Sounded like a regular darned war." He raised an arm. "Out yonder. Maybe six, eight shots, then silence."

Bill did not waste time. "Saddle up. If Kimball

has run onto the bushwhackers, maybe he can use a few extra hands."

No one told the *cosinero,* and he had been slamming pots and pans inside the cookshack so had not heard any distant gunfire, but when he opened the door to look out he saw the entire riding crew except for Paul Franklyn heading out of the yard. He stopped, squinted, then slowly reddened as he stepped out onto the porch and said, "I'll be damned — he was in such a hurry for dinner, now there he goes with the whole crew. That damned Bill Burton would drive a man to drink."

He suddenly opened his eyes wider, lost the expression of annoyance, turned and marched back inside, rolling up a sleeve as he went toward the flour-barrel.

The day was bright, and away from trees it was hot. Summer would not actually arrive for another month, but there was a definite hot spell over the high ridge range country today. It had unusual humidity to it, perhaps because of the diaphanous veil which seemed to be fixed into place across the entire breadth and depth of the heavens. There was also a thin skiff of dirty-looking thin clouds over in the east, not very many, and they did not appear to be moving, but they were over there, and when viewed in conjunction with that sky-high veil and humidity, it was easy to predict rainfall within the next twenty-four hours or so, if anyone had been sufficiently interested to look up.

Bill didn't, neither did Bud Fisk or the other Weatherford rangemen. If Walt had been closer to Fisk he would have said something sarcastic about a gun-battle erupting up in the same area he and Bud had scoured over last night, until cold and doubt had turned them back.

It would have been an unnecessary reminder. Bud loped beside Bill with his eyes pinched nearly closed and his jaw set in a disagreeable way. If those bushwhackers had indeed had a camp up there, and he had ridden past, the wisest thing he could do right now was not open his mouth.

Bill halted eventually, waited until the others piled up around him, and sat with a screwed-up face squinting ahead. There was not a horseman in sight. In fact there was nothing in sight, not even cattle. And there was a deep silence, as though there probably had been nothing up there, gunmen or anything else.

Walt Poole risked a guess. "Maybe they was havin' a runnin' fight, and maybe they went into the foothills or eastward."

Bud said, "They wouldn't run eastward, Walt. That's open country."

The rangeboss agreed with this and lifted his rein-hand. They set a fresh course directly for the nearest low hills, came around a rolling high rib of land in a swinging lope, and nearly rode into three dismounted men leaning over a fourth man.

Guns appeared instantly on both sides, then

one of the dismounted men, shirt-tail out, face red and sweaty, yelped. "Hold it. Hold it for Chris'sake. It's the Weatherford outfit."

The rangecrew swung off and walked ahead trailing their reins. There was a man on the ground, flat on his back and motionless. Bud Fisk shouldered past and looked. "George Kimball," he said sharply.

One of the three possemen did not raise his head when he confirmed it. "The sheriff. We spooked some fellers out of a chaparral thicket, and George went after 'em like a mountain lion. He yelled for them to halt. One of 'em turned, usin' both hands while his horse was on the run and his reins was looped, and shot George out of the saddle. We had a hell of a runnin' fight of it for a spell, then they split up in the foothills an' we lost 'em."

Bill Burton stood gazing downward. George Kimball had been hit flush in the centre of the chest. He had been dead about the time he landed on the ground. It took a little getting accustomed to, looking at George dead after all those years of seeing him alive.

Finally, Bill raised his head. They had plenty of daylight left, but a lot of time had been lost. He curtly said, "Get a-horseback. Bud, take a couple of riders and scout along the base of the hills — and for Chris'sake be careful; that bastard is a marksman. Walt, take a couple of fellers and scour the north foothills up near the mountain-slope. You be careful too. He'll shoot you off your horse from ambush if he can. The rest of you come with me. We're goin' to fan out and brush these damned foothills until we flush something."

The fleeing men had no choice but to continue to flee, but Bill did not doubt but that they would be doing that in any case. What he had in mind was riding them down; not pushing the horses beyond what they could tolerate, and keep doing it. Sooner or later those hard-riding mankillers would have to rest their animals.

George had been with posses when they had done this same thing years back. He had seen it where posses making a horse-race out of a pursuit had had to give up because of exhausted mounts.

The foothills were roughly five miles in depth, and they were ideal for ambushes, but Bill Burton did not worry about that. For two hours anyway he was certain there would be no danger of a bushwhacking, and after the two hours had been passed without sighting any fleeing horsemen, he was cold-bloodedly willing to risk getting someone shot if he could bring the rest of the riders down upon those mankillers.

Bill Burton wanted someone's hide, preferably with their blood on it, and those who knew Bill best could have predicted how he would react to a near-killing and an actual killing on Weatherford range.

The possemen mingled with Burton's riders. Once, when they all halted to allow Bud and his companions to catch up, one of the townsmen asked if Bill thought it likely that the men they were seeking might head for Ridgefield.

Bill did not think so. What those bush-whackers needed very desperately right now was not a town, but hundreds of miles of open country to make excellent haste in.

Walt Poole came along, angling up-country from the lower foothills. They widened their sweeping line now, covering the entire of the hills. Bill was in the centre of the line, beyond talking distance of the riders nearest him, but not out of sight of them. It was just as well; Bill Burton had not been this coldly, deadly angry in more years than he could have recalled. He would not keep a conversation going even if there had been someone close by to talk to.

The sun was behind them, descending slowly and acquiring a rusty red colour. They encountered some Weatherford cattle once, and allowed them to sift through their miles-deep skirmish line, and shortly before reaching the stage-road which went southward to Ridgefield they spooked a band of pronghorns. The fleet little animals out-distanced the horsemen effort-lessly, and still could have done it if the riders had been running their mounts.

Eight

Into the Night

When Bill was satisfied they were not going to meet the bushwhackers west of the roadway, he sent one of the townsmen southward to Ridgefield for a wagon, told him to go back for George Kimball, and haul him to town, and for him to tell the councilmen in Ridgefield what he and his riders were doing, and the direction they were riding in. Then Bill saw Bud looking almost stoically at him and said, "You got an idea, or are you just gettin' hungry?"

Bud overlooked the irritability in his friend. "You could have told that feller to use the wireless in town and notify the towns ahead."

Bill nodded. He could indeed have done that, but he had a personal reason for not doing it. Maybe, as they rode onward, Bud guessed something about this; both of them had been on the range a long time. Both of them had done things few younger riders had ever had to do.

The sun was high and there was heat. Bill did not set a gruelling pace, but he did not allow any stops either until mid-afternoon, then he halted long enough for the horses to tank up at a creek, and afterwards sent Walt and Jess high up along the northward sidehill to stay parallel while looking for movement on ahead.

It was a good thing he did that. The sun was beginning to sink when the wizened, sinewy cowboy came down the mountain-side on an angling lope, caught up and pointed dead ahead. "Cowcamp up ahead about five, six miles."

Bill accepted this scrap of information. They would be on the range of the Brewster outfit by the time they got ahead that far.

Then Jess said, "They're raising dust all over hell up there, chasin' loose horses."

That hit Bill hard. He and Jess exchanged a look, and the rangeboss swore. Jess, evidently having long ago arrived at the same notion, bobbed his head.

Bill wig-wagged with his hat and set his riders in a forward lope and held them to it until they were within sight of the cowcamp wagon, and the men on foot down there, then they dropped down to a long-legged walk.

The Brewster rangeboss was not there but his tophand was. Bill knew the man, not well, but well enough. As he sat his saddle amid the excitement the tophand said, "We had some horses stole and the rest turned loose. We just finished catchin' the loose ones."

Bill looked at the ten or twelve horses back inside their rope corral, then looked down at the sun-bronzed tall man and said, "Three fellers, Ira?"

The tophand made a wide gesture with both arms. "Never seen 'em, Bill. We was gettin' ready to strike camp and was workin' over here loadin' the wagon when someone yelled, and hell there was loose horses goin' in all directions."

Burton exchanged a look with Bud Fisk, then he said, "Ira, we need fresh animals," and as the tophand stood looking up at Burton with a puzzled, testy stare, Bill explained curtly. "There's three of them. They shot one of my riders yesterday, and this morning when George Kimball went after them — they killed him."

The tophand's expression changed. "Killed Kimball?"

"Yeah." Bill gestured. "These fellers with us are part of George's posse. They can tell you the rest of it. Ira, we got to have those horses."

Bill was dismounting as he said this. When he stepped ahead past his horse the tophand was looking among the mounted men. One of them who knew the tophand said, "It's gospel truth, Ira. We had a runnin' fight. One of them bastards shot George off his horse, then they split up."

The tophand turned slowly. "All right," he said to Bill Burton, and raised his voice to the man back by the wagon. "Lend a hand," he called. "Move fast!"

When Burton's riders had fresh animals there

were four left, but two of them were harness-horses to pull the camp wagon, and when Ira wanted to go with the manhunters Bill talked him out of it. He did not need any more men, he told the tophand, he needed more time.

They left the cowcamp at a loose jog until their borrowed animals had been warmed out a little, then they boosted them over into a lope and held them to it for several miles. Then, when Walt Poole joined them on his Weatherford horse, Bill told him to take Jeff and scout for fresh sign. Two of those bushwhackers were probably angling away from the third fellow.

It was a sound guess. But what Walt and Jess found was not the tracks of the two they were looking for, but the fresh tracks of one rider heading due eastward in a dead run.

Bill smiled about that and told Bud Fisk they had this one; not even a race-horse could keep up that gait for long. Then they all rode together never hastening but never slackening off either.

The sun sank, daylight lingered another two hours, and Jess, who was a good tracker, finally threw up his hands; visibility was down to about one yard. He swung off and led his horse, reading sign a yard at a time, but an hour later when there was sooty darkness he had to give up entirely. However, he had worked a few things out from those tracks, and told Bill he was fairly sure the man they were chasing was not too far ahead, possibly two or three miles was all, and that he would have to rest his stolen horse or end up on foot, and in either case, if they kept due east the way the bushwhacker had been riding most of the afternoon they would find him.

Bill sent Jess on ahead with a warning to be very careful, because if the man they were shagging was the one who never missed, not even from the back of a moving horse, he just might be able to see in the dark too.

Jess smiled to show brown teeth, said nothing and rode away.

One of the possemen left them shortly after Jess had departed. He was unaccustomed to hard exertion and was worn out. The Weatherford riders watched him head southward without comment, but with a unanimous feeling that the departing posseman was an epitome of what ailed all who lived in towns.

Walt rode up beside Bill and dryly said, "If the other two fellers are in the mountains, they'll feel safe enough to make a camp. Come morning, we'll be east of 'em, well ahead."

Bill nodded. "Come morning we'll look for sign. If it isn't up ahead, then we'll circle back until we find 'em." Then Bill looked steadily at the lanky Montanan. "You hungry, Walt?"

The cowboy skinned thin lips back from big, square white teeth. "Naw. Neither are the other fellers. But we'll be hungry when this is over."

They exchanged a grin and Bill rode ahead, letting his borrowed horse slog along at a fast walk on a loose rein.

A horse lamed up. It was being ridden by

83

another of the townsmen and he was not very happy about having to turn back. The cowboys sympathised with him; evidently there were *some* townsmen who didn't give out on a hard trail.

They now had only one of Sheriff Kimball's possemen still with them. When Bill held up his hand for a halt and they all sat still, listening for sounds on ahead, that remaining townsman eased up beside Bud Fisk and said, "We'll never find him in the dark."

The tophand's reply was dry. "It's been known to happen, friend."

But they heard nothing, so Bill led off again, and this time they rode for a full mile before Walt Poole raised his gloved hand for another halt. This time, they heard the walking horse coming toward them.

It was the sinewy, nut-brown older rangeman. He hauled up facing Bill and said, "There's a horse up ahead in a swale. He ain't hobbled and I didn't get close enough to see whether he's been rode — but if he's someone's loose-stock, he wouldn't be out here by himself."

All the rangemen agreed with that in silence. Bill asked how far ahead, and Jess made a little indifferent gesture. "Walkin' distance."

They all swung off. The townsman volunteered to mind the horses, so they handed over their reins and started walking.

Jess was slightly ahead. There was a moon on the rise and plenty of stars to aid limited visibility, but they did not see the trees upon the edge of the onward swale until they were within a hundred feet or so of them. Jess led them in among the shadows of pines, halted and pointed.

The horse was down below cropping grass, and as Jess had said, he was not hobbled, which meant that he could run away any time he felt like it, or when someone approached him. They could not even make out his colour, but he was tall and rangy, and that made them hopeful, because the bushwhacker had to have had an animal of this calibre to cover as much ground as he had covered, as fast as he had covered it.

Bill said, "Circle around him. Don't let him run, or wherever the feller is he's goin' to hear it."

They were all seasoned at this sort of thing. By the time the tall horse knew there were men out there with him in the night, they were beginning to close in on him from all sides. He threw up his head and squared around for flight, but there was a two-legged critter everywhere he looked.

Bill took the initiative. He began quietly, soothingly talking to the horse as he took his time walking up to him. He stopped each time the horse fidgeted, waited, then started walking again. The horse could have broken past, but being a stock-horse he thought in terms of lariats when men were coming toward him, and even though the man coming closer had no rope in his hands, the horse was still a stock-animal; the

85

habits of a lifetime did not disappear this quickly.

Bill did not want to catch the horse, he simply wanted to look for sweat-stains and the Brewster mark. It was there, a Rafter B on the left shoulder. The sweat-stains were also there. The horse was a bay, fairly young judging by his chin, and not really excitable, although as Bill walked slowly around him he acted as though he could be spooked without much effort.

Then the two-legged critter turned abruptly and walked away leaving the horse looking after him in puzzlement.

Bud Fisk was waiting when Bill came back and said, "All right. I got no idea why he turned the horse loose, but the son of a bitch is around here somewhere. He sure isn't goin' far on foot."

They went in search of the others, then started back where they had left the horses and found the townsman in a mood of powerful curiosity. Bill explained what they had found, and the townsman surprised them all by saying, "I know this country up here as well as I know the back of my hand. Hunt bucks up through here every autumn. If he's got a camp, I can find it. But wasn't the horse even hobbled?"

Bill shook his head, gazing at the townsman. "Standin' loose in a grassy place. I know what you're thinking; I wondered the same thing. Why would a fugitive deliberately turn loose the only horse he's got. Right now, we want to find

86

the son of a bitch. After that we can maybe ask him why he did that. Let's go. You know the country, you lead off — be quiet and be damned careful."

The townsman stood a moment in thought. He was a shockle-headed husky man, younger than Bill or Bud. In fact he was probably younger than any of the other men as well. His name was Eb Torrance and he worked at the wagon-works in Ridgefield. Bill and perhaps several of the other rangemen thought they had seen him around town, but they did not know him. Right at this moment that did not matter as the posseman struck out, finally, after the horses had been hobbled, the cinches loosened, and the rangemen had arrived at their individual ideas about what it might mean, closing in on a bush-whacker who might even know he was being fol-lowed this close.

Bud Fisk told Bill he did not believe the man had any idea they were this close to him, and Walt dryly dissented. "If he wasn't blind this afternoon, and was lookin' back a little, he could have spotted us any time we was ridin' clear of the hills."

No one replied to that. There were a number of things which required answers, but they were not going to get any answers until they found the bushwhacker, and perhaps they would not get answers even then. Nor did that matter right at this moment.

The posseman was a careful, cautious individual, and it was obvious almost at once that he did indeed know the country they were moving into.

Once, he paused and softly informed the men crowding close that his guess was that the fugitive would be on high ground, probably where there were sheltering trees; a place where, come daylight, he would command a good view in all directions.

No one disagreed, so the posseman began angling around the top of the swale where the horse was grazing, but on the far side of it until he could point to a stand of pines on the north side of the swale.

He said, "Spread out. If we can get around them trees, and he's in there —"

Bill gave quiet orders. Jess took a younger man and started up the higher slope northward. Walt and another man waited until they saw Bud and Bill break away eastward, then Walt jerked his head and went southward. He hurried because he and his companion would have the farthest distance to walk, but Walt was split a long way up the middle and could take wide strides. His companion was less endowed so he had to scurry to keep up, but he did not open his mouth to complain.

It was turning cold, and although the moon was high now that thickening veil of high overcast diffused the moonlight so that visibility was not very good.

Bud Fisk was standing perfectly still studying

the line of trees the townsman had thought might be where their prey was resting when he thought he distantly heard horses up the slope, and looked around for Bill, but Burton was not close enough to speak to and was still moving, so Bud waited a moment longer, did not hear that sound again, decided it had been his imagination, and struck out again.

They were attempting to do as they had done with the bay horse, get completely around the stand of timber, except that up here the trees did not grow in a clump, they were scattered out for perhaps three or four hundred yards in the watery moonlight.

Bud finally got up close to the rangeboss, and Bill halted to lift out his sixgun. He was looking intently at the nearest trees and turned when Bud stepped up to say, "Wait. Give Walt time to get into position."

Bill nodded without speaking for a long time, then he used his sixgun barrel as a pointer. "If we can get up in there we'll have protection. Careful now."

They started walking again, more slowly this time, and had almost reached the nearest timber when there was a rattle of rocks up the northward slope, and farther east. Bill cursed under his breath. Someone had stepped into an area of loose stones.

Bud stood stock-still, scarcely breathing, his eyes fixed on the area dead ahead of them. For a long time there was not another sound after the last of those rolling rocks stopped moving.

Bill very slowly raised his left hand and pointed. Bud had to lean slightly to see that far through the darkness and standing timber. Then he saw it — stealthy movement from southward in among the trees. For five seconds he held his breath. By then the silent, shadowy movement was recognisable as a man. He was moving with an effort, only about a foot or two at a time, and he was bent forward.

Bill very slowly lowered his left arm, and like the tophand, neither moved nor looked away from the shadowy silhouette. He saw the carbine finally, when the shadow reached the northern-most trees and halted, peering up the slope where those rocks had broken free.

Bud started to sink to one knee, but Bill caught his arm and held him still. The shadow was looking northward, but if he turned his head slightly he would see Bud moving. He was within sixgun range.

They waited, unheeding of the cold, the silence, the overcast, of everything but the bent-forward shadow with the carbine, and when the man finally inched ahead a few more steps and was in front of his backgrounding trees, hold-ing his Winchester across his body in both hands now, Bill regripped his handgun, ready to raise it, when a sharp-sounding voice spoke from the east, giving a two-worded command.

"Don't move!"

Bill saw the shadow start to unbend, and

tipped up his sixgun, gave the identical order from the stranger's left side, then cocked his Colt.

The man's head turned slowly from right to left. They were on both sides of him.

From southward, in among the trees and not very far from where the stranger had been, before he had crept northward after that rattle of loose stones, a dry voice said, "Let go of that carbine!"

Walt had one of those dry voices that would have been recognisable under any circumstances. He spoke again because the stranger did not obey him. "You drop it, mister, or I'll drop you!"

Finally, Bud Fisk sank to one knee, raised his Colt and hauled back the dog. Again, the sound of a gun being cocked sounded through the hush.

Bud said, *"Drop it!"*

The stranger had had all the time a man would need, even a slow-witted man, to realise he was surrounded by men willing to kill him if he did not drop his Winchester.

He let it fall to the ground.

Nine

The Deadshot

The last man to come up was that posseman from Ridgefield, and because something was strongly on his mind, even though he saw them all facing their captive, he blurted out an apology for slipping in the loose rocks.

No one even looked at him. Their captive was a sharp-faced man with features like a fox, and lank blond hair which hung from beneath an old grey broad-brimmed hat. He would have been tall if he had been standing straight, but he was sloping forward slightly as Jess lifted away his holstered Colt, spat aside, and moved back.

He was a young man, a head taller than Jess who had disarmed him, and when Bill said, "Are you hurt?" the captive considered Burton for several seconds before slowly nodding his head. "Got bucked off," he said. "Twice. Hurt my knee the first time. The last time hurt my back."

Walt had a question. "From that big bay horse down in the glade?"

The sharp-featured man turned to look back at the Montanan. "You see any other horse around here, mister?"

Walt grinned. "Next time you steal a horse, take one that's already under saddle."

Bill got the conversation back where he wanted it to be. "Where are your partners?"

The fox-faced man said, "I don't know what you're talkin' about. Who the hell are you, anyway?"

Bill Burton was in no mood for this. He pointed back through the trees and said, "Jess, hunt up his camp." Then he lowered his arm in the direction of a punky old deadfall and gave the bushwhacker an order. "Sit down." The fox-faced man hitched over to the log, thankful for a chance to take weight off his injured knee and back. Bill said, "Walt, you and the posseman go fetch up our horses."

Finally, Bill looked at Bud Fisk, and the top-hand was looking steadily back. Now Bud knew why Bill had not wanted any telegrams sent ahead, and now, too, he understood why Bill had not showed annoyance or disgust in his face when two of the possemen had had to turn back. Bill intended to see this bushwhacker killed on the spot.

The rangeboss said, "What's your name?" and when the sullen, fox-faced man said, "John Smith, what's yours?" Bill hit him so hard the bushwhacker was lifted bodily and sent sprawling upon the far side of the log.

Bud showed nothing on his face as he went around, got the man onto his feet, helped him to the log and quietly said, "Don't do it again."

Bill was rubbing sore knuckles with the opposite hand when he repeated the question, and this time the bushwhacker took Bud's advice. "Rob Moore."

Bill nodded. He had already known this was one of the Moores; he had not known which one. "Where are the other two?" he asked, still massaging his sore knuckles. This time the answer was delayed while the bushwhacker watched Jess return from deeper within the trees and toss a pair of saddlebags upon the ground.

"I got no idea where they are," Rob Moore said, raising his eyes to the rangeboss's face. "What difference does it make, anyhow?"

"That lawman you shot back yonder is dead."

"I never shot no lawman."

"And you never tried to shoot your cousin either, did you?" Bill spat and looked stonily at the seated man.

The bushwhacker raised a hand to his beard-stubbled face. "All's I know, mister, is that me'n my brothers was in camp when some fellers come bustin' up at us yellin' an' wavin' guns. We run for it. There was some shooting. What the hell — what would you have done if —"

"Maybe the same thing you did, but I wouldn't have come so far to kill my own kin."

Rob Moore's pale eyes lingered upon the rangeboss's face. "Yes you would have, mister. That sorry bastard murdered our paw. You'd have done exactly as we done. Any man would have."

Bud said, "How do you murder a man who's just shot a horse from under you and is comin' at you with his shotgun?"

Rob Moore shifted his attention. "That's *his* story. It's a lie from start to finish."

"But there was a dead horse in the yard," stated Bud.

The bushwhacker blinked, then said, "Sure there was. Paw got off one shot after —"

"After he'd been hit through the heart?"

"He had his finger on the trigger."

"You weren't there. How do you know what happened?"

Rob Moore's brows dropped. "You wasn't there neither, mister."

Bud agreed to that. "I wasn't, but I know someone who was there."

"Who?"

"Your cousin."

Moore sneered. "Crap," he said, in scathing disdain. "He's dead. Now you try an' prove what happened."

Bill Burton flexed his sore hand as he said, "He's not dead. But I guess we know where you three bastards were when we buried that canvas with the straw inside it, don't we?"

Rob Moore stared hard at Bill.

Walt and the posseman named Torrance returned riding a horse each and leading the other horses. They tied the animals among the trees, and Walt picked up the saddlebags, opened them and spilled their contents upon the ground. Among the strictly personal items such as a razor, soap, a ball of fishline with a snelled hook embedded in it, and some extra clothing, was one of those dodgers Bill had brought back from Ridgefield with him. It was folded, worn and dog-eared. When Walt spread it out everyone but Bill Burton and Rob Moore leaned to look. Bill turned on his heel, went to the nearest horse, took down the lariat and walked back holding the coiled rope in his left hand.

"For bushwhacking Paul and killin' Sheriff Kimball," he said quietly, and watched the fox-faced man turn pale. "Or you can take a chance and run for it."

Moore said, "I'm hurt. Listen, mister, what we done we was justified in doing. That bastard killed our paw. His paw tried to steal our cattle range."

Bill wagged his head. "I don't care about what led up to any of this. All I care about is that you tried to kill Paul Franklyn, from ambush, like any other damned bushwhacker, and you did kill the sheriff. That's all. Stand up."

Moore did not move off the log. He turned from face to face, and only one showed any emotion. The town posseman was aghast. He was staring at the rangeboss as though he could not believe what he was witnessing.

Walt Poole tapped Torrance on the shoulder and jerked his head. "Maybe you'd better get a-horseback, friend, and head for home."

The posseman twisted from beneath Walt's

hand and said, "Mister Burton — you can't do this. Good gawd he's got a trial coming."

Jess spoke sharply. "He'll get a trial. You better do as Walt said — head for home."

Torrance looked around. There was not a sympathetic look among those rangemen. He swallowed with an effort. He had heard about things like this happening out away from the towns in cow country, but he had never expected to be part of it. He dredged up all the things he had heard in an attempt to dissuade the range-boss. "You'll be as guilty of murder as he is, if you hang him, Mister Burton. Besides that, it'll get out; folks will hear about it an' the law'll be lookin' for you."

Bill turned on the posseman. "You got no lawman, remember? One of these sons of bitches shot him. Like Walt said — get on that Brewster horse and ride back down to town."

"But good gawd, Mister Burton —" He let it trail off into silence. Walt was leading a horse over. He looked from the horse to Walt Poole, then back to Bill Burton.

Jess tapped him on the chest and pushed a lined, sun-darkened, malevolent face up close. "Who's goin' to tell 'em down in Ridgefield what happened? Partner, if they come after Bill, there's four of us will be left, and we'll come for you — and so help me, we'll find you." Jess eased back a little and softened his tone of voice. "Get on that horse. You got a secret all of your own. *Get on the damned horse!*"

The posseman made one final attempt to intercede when he said, "It'll be on your consciences as long as you live."

He might as well have been addressing a stone, or one of the big trees where they were standing. Walt flipped up the reins and made a peremptory gesture. The posseman climbed astride, agitatedly gathered the reins, evened them up, and turned to ride out of the trees. Not a word was said. The rangemen and their white-faced prisoner watched him.

He got out into the ghostly, diaphanous moonlight and was starting to twist for a final rearward look, when the gunshot flashed from up the slope, and before the muzzleblast-thunder died the posseman was still twisting in his saddle, but more drunkenly now, then he dropped and the horse ran.

By instinct, the rangemen dropped for cover. The man sitting on the log opened his mouth to yell, and Jess caught him from behind, wrenched him over backwards off the log and shoved a cocked Colt into his face. "One gawddamned sound. Just one!" The gasping bushwhacker did not move until Jess had removed the gun and gave the bushwhacker a hard shove as he said, "Don't you move out of this spot."

Bud Fisk calmly spoke from behind a big pinetree. "North and a little west, maybe a hundred yards or better up there."

No one answered. No one expected the gunman to still be in the same position. Walt crawled gingerly out where the posseman was lying flat out on his back, rocked the inert body a couple of times, raised up enough to see the wound, then crawled back to cover. From the dark shadows he said, "I'll tell you boys something. This one we got ain't the marksman. He's up yonder somewhere. He hit that town-feller right through the head, and that, by gawd, is about the best shootin' even for daylight I ever seen."

Bill waited until the surprise had passed, then hissed for someone to move their horses deeper into the timber. Jess growled at someone near him in the darkness and went toward the agitated animals.

The tophand, who had always been an imperturbable man, offered the rangeboss some advice. "There's still two of 'em, and sure as hell one of 'em is goin' to try and get around behind us."

Bill knew that. He also knew something else; unless they did not care about the life of their brother — which they certainly did care about or they would not have tried to stampede the Weatherford crew, but would have simply kept on riding — he had high hand in this game. He could hang Rob Moore in plain sight of his brothers unless they came up to scratch.

When Jess returned from hiding the horse and passed Bill he asked a question. "They can't see us in here. Maybe one of us could run for it. What do you think?"

"Sit down," the rangeboss replied. "Wait. That's open country south of us, and come daylight if they're still northward in the trees, we got a better chance than they got; there's five of us."

Bill did not enlarge upon it. He did not have to. As the men sought to get comfortable and keep warm, they knew that someone, either from town once George Kimball was down there, or the Brewster riding crew, would come along. It was not possible to stir up as much trouble as those bushwhackers had stirred up without having half the countryside aroused, armed and riding.

From up the north slope a man called forth in a deep, rough voice. "Let him loose. Let him ride out 'n there and we'll head out. You hear me?"

Bill delayed his answer, then gave it. "Come get him."

"We will, if you don't let him ride out'n there. If we come after you, you'll wish to hell we hadn't."

Bill called back. "You better hurry. We got the rope all set to haul him up with."

There was silence after that. Walt took one of the younger riders and went southward through the timber until he could see down across the swale where the bay horse had been. He was no longer out there. Perhaps the gunshot had spooked him. It did not matter. Walt pointed to a big tree for his companion, got behind one just as large close by, and grinned in the sooty gloom

The younger cowboy grinned back, but without the same enthusiasm. He had seen two dead men today, knew for a fact one of the bushwhackers he could not hear or see was a dead-shot, and regardless of their numbers and their sheltering big trees, would have given several months' wages just to be back on Weatherford range hunting cattle or even dunging out the horse-barn.

Jess sat up after a while and considered their prisoner. Rob Moore was still on his back, taking Jess's warning about not moving very seriously. Jess wagged his head. "We'll shoot two an' hang one."

Moore did not reply. He had his head rolled as far to the left as he could turn it and was staring up through the darkness of the north slope.

Bud Fisk watched the rangeboss worry a chew off his plug and work it into a comfortable position inside his cheek. Bud did not chew, he had tried it once as a youngster; it had made him so sick he had never tried it again. But Bud smoked, and right now he would have enjoyed a cigarette, but made no move to roll one. When Bill saw Bud watching him he said, "Daylight in about two hours." Until that moment Bud had not thought of this night ending. Now, he eased around among the trees until he could scan the eastward horizon, and sure enough there was a pale grey streak all along the uneven far edge of the world. He crawled back and got into position again. "Whatever they got in mind they'll do it soon," he said, and Bill offered a curt response. "Well, that's what we're waiting for."

The cold was bitter, and while the men were dressed for it, and had coats behind their cantles over where the horses were tied, no one was eager to walk over there. For all they knew, by now those bushwhackers were in close enough to see a man standing up.

Something else was in their minds; there was a man out there in the darkness who could shoot men off moving horses like other men shot whiskey bottles off stumps.

They preferred to be a little cold, without moving, and, as Bill had said, they could out-wait the bushwhackers. But waiting was tiresome, particularly in the cold.

Ten

Death at Dawn

Someone pitched a rock in among the trees. Bud Fisk wryly wagged his head. That was something a greenhorn would do.

No one fired in the direction from which the rock had been thrown, and Jess quietly said, "At least they ain't froze yet."

Bill chewed, spat, watched the uphill slope begin to brighten a tad, and looked around. His men were motionless, watching and listening. Bud Fisk had turned up his collar and buttoned it and was blowing on his gloved hands.

Walt Poole was watching the open glade, and out there away from the mountain-side daylight was making a better showing. Walt's visibility improved by the moment. He watched his young companion for a few moments, then had his attention pulled back around by faint movement on their left.

He gently hoisted the gun in his hand, then watched as a female skunk came out of a leafy burrow followed in single file by four exact duplications of her, in miniature. The mother

103

skunk was probably taking her brood to water, but as far as Walt knew there was none around. But small animals did not require much water, sometimes dew which had collected in a shallow place would be sufficient.

The mother skunk abruptly stopped, raised her ferret-like face and sifted faint air-currents as though she had detected an unwelcome scent. A skunk rarely gave ground, and a mother skunk with babies would not yield an inch, she would attack, hissing, teeth bared, ears flattened, and if that did not discourage an interloper she'd swap ends and spray. If that spray struck human hide it burned; it also was just about impossible to wash off, the aroma lingered for days. Walt had been in bunkhouses with men who had been hit by skunk spray.

He sought the reason for her suddenly defensive stance and saw nothing for a long while, not until the younger man behind his nearby tree whispered hoarsely for Walt to watch the trees east of them and over the edge of their ridge a few yards. He had seen movement back up there. It was too large to be a predator, unless it was a bear.

Walt shifted position and watched, but was unable to make out either movement or a silhouette. He nevertheless shifted position a little more, flattened against the soft needles, and shoved out his gun-hand.

He saw and heard nothing.

Behind them, back through the trees, Bill

Burton was farther east than the other riders, and he did not see anything, but he faintly heard the whisper-soft breaking of dry pine needles, a sound which continued, and which brought him up alert and wary because the cadence was that of a man, or some other heavy critter which moved a step at a time.

He swung to see if Bud had also detected anything. Bud was rubbing his gloved hands together and looking up the north slope. Bill began to move a little at a time. Jess and Rob Moore saw him do this, and quickened to life. Moore twisted to look eastward. There was still nothing to see.

Jess twisted half around eastward without making a sound, and because he was close to the ground the movement was not even observed by Bud Fisk who was upon the opposite side of the punky log where he could see Jess.

Bill got a large pine-tree directly in front, and moved very carefully up to it. He could not see eastward as long as he remained behind the tree, but whoever was out there could not see him moving, either.

He very carefully got belly-down, eased his head around — and saw a man's shadowy silhouette blend with a distant tree, pass from sight momentarily, then emerge stealthily moving southward in the direction of other large trees. Bill squirmed out a little farther. Now, Bud was watching. So was Jess and their prisoner. None of them moved, but Bud and Jess brought their guns to the ready position. Moore was rigid; he appeared ready to cry out, but moments passed and he did not do it.

From southward, down where Walt and his companions were, there was not a sound as the sky steadily brightened from sooty grey to lighter grey. Down there, visibility had improved sufficiently for the Weatherford men to have an excellent view of that glade where the bay horse had been, and for miles beyond in all directions. Walt, while still interested in what had startled the mother skunk, was no longer watching her. Neither was his companion. They were both peering eastward where the younger rangeman had seen movement.

Finally, Bud saw the man. He was holding a saddlegun in both hands across his upper body as he surreptitiously slipped from tree to tree, like an Indian.

He was not close enough for Walt's sixgun, and neither Walt nor his partner had carbines. But Walt was satisfied that the bushwhacker would eventually turn toward them; he had to if his intention was to scout through the trees for his enemies — and his brother.

The younger cowboy was sweating under his heavy attire, but Walt was perfectly calm — cold still, but calm. He was no longer conscious of the cold though.

Once he turned aside to expectorate, then he faced ahead and waited.

Bill lost the man among the southward trees

and began to worry that the bushwhacker might get behind Walt and the other rangeman down there. He turned, got up onto one knee against his tree and speculated about his chances if he boldly moved.

The other bushwhacker had to be skulking somewhere not too far away. Bill turned, jerked his head to indicate the westerly drift of timber, and waited until Bud understood and switched positions to keep watch in the other direction. It was the best they could do, and if that other killer was northward they would all be watching in the wrong direction.

Without warning a horse nickered from back among the trees westerly. They all turned swiftly, except Bud who was already facing that direction. The horse did not repeat it, but he shifted position and they could all hear that. He would have turned to face something; they would have liked to have seen which direction he was facing, but he was not visible because of the timber.

Bud eased over and got behind a big tree facing westerly. Bill guessed the tophand's intention, but turned back in the opposite direction looking for the other one, who was now lost to sight southward. Bill turned his head toward Jess and pointed to Moore. In a whisper he said, "Stay with this one," then he started to move. One second later a sixgun exploded southward, down where Walt and his partner were, and two seconds later a carbine slashed back its higher-pitched snarl.

This time, two hand-guns sounded, and echoes bounced off tall trees in all directions making the location of those men impossible to determine unless a person already knew where they were.

Bill waited, and when the carbine slashed back another venomous explosion, Bill ducked and ran for another tree. He did this five times, then sank flat and tried to see where the black-powder smoke was rising. There was enough of it, but it was too diffused among the trees. He guessed about where Walt and the other Weatherford man were, within fifty or so feet, but the bush-whacker had moved after his first shot and probably had done it again after his second shot. He knew now there were a pair of rangemen southward preventing him from getting around behind the other man. Bill gambled that he had no idea another rangeman was north of him on his left side, and moved forward, half crawling, half sprinting. He had the acrid scent of gun-smoke in his face when he finally saw a blur of movement, as though the bushwhacker were retreating back the way he had come, which was toward Bill but east of him a dozen or so yards.

Behind Bill, two gunshots rang out so close together they almost sounded as one, except that the first one, by a second, had been made by a Winchester.

Then there was a flurry of gunshots back there, five or six in rapid succession, three of which had been fired from a carbine.

Bill was finally sweating, and beyond the trees that brightening sky was dull grey instead of rose-pink. No one noticed, but the veil they had noticed days before was thicker now and much lower to the earth, like a vast, gossamer blanket of soiled atmosphere.

Bill wanted to crawl eastward in order to be closer when the man who was pulling back from the south passed him. He wanted to, but he did not do it. He was within sixgun range, he thought, and made himself lie there waiting.

The bushwhacker appeared almost as though he were a ghost, moving back in a soft-flowing series of stealthy glides. He was looking south-westerly, in the direction he had unexpectedly encountered Walt and the other rangeman.

Bill lifted his Colt, placed his left hand against a rough network of pine bark, eased the right hand across his left wrist, cocked the sixgun, and waited. The route of the bushwhacker's with-drawal would take him directly between two big trees which were about fifteen feet apart. Bill took long aim at the centre of that place, let his breath out very slowly, and when the ambusher moved, Bill fired.

The bushwhacker's carbine, being held slightly to one side as the man retreated, shat-tered and swung violently, striking the man who had been holding it along the ribs and upper body. The wooden stock disintegrated, the man staggered drunkenly, then fell. The gun was torn from his hands and spun ten feet through the air before it fell.

Bill had not tried to do that, but now, as the bushwhacker struggled to reach tree-shelter, he was obviously dazed and only belatedly reached down for his Colt. Bill yelled at him to stop, but the man, driven now by instinct, ignored the shout, tumbled in behind a big tree, and Bill squeezed off his second shot without being very hopeful. It was close; tree-bark flew, a long, splinter of wet wood was torn away, and Bill lowered his gun to reload as he watched ahead.

The fight to the west, over in the vicinity of the horses, had ended. There was no way for Bill, or the other men who had engaged the man in front of Bill, to know how it had ended.

After the initial fight, and Bill Burton had reloaded, he had a while for calm thought. If the man he had shot at was the marksman, then Bill was still in great peril, but at least the bush-whacker no longer had his carbine, and in a sixgun fight it was not always the most accurate man who scored; sixguns were not accurate from a distance, which made it more nearly a fair fight now, as Bill eased up, cocked the Colt in his sweaty palm, then waited.

The silence was deafening. It was also har-rowing. Bill had his back to the west. If that other bushwhacker had survived back yonder and could get close enough to look past, he would see Burton's exposed back. Unless of course Jess and Bud were facing him, in which

110

case he could still see Bill's back, but his immediate peril would be two capable men looking for him.

Bill decided to try shouting. He called to the man behind the big tree to come out, unarmed. There was no answer. He told the bushwhacker he could not survive, and that each passing moment was working against him.

There was still no answer.

Unexpectedly, Walt Poole spoke without more than raising his voice a notch. He was somewhere south of the man in front of Bill, and obviously he was moving northward too, which meant he would be behind the bushwhacker shortly. He said, "I'm goin' to bust your head like a rotten pumpkin unless you drop that gun and stand up."

Bill heard movement behind the tree as the desperate bushwhacker swiftly turned to seek Walt below and behind him. He did not say a word, nor did he stand up and drop his gun.

Walt spoke again, closer this time and more nearly behind the cornered killer. "This is the last time — stand up and drop that gun!"

The bushwhacker had Bill in front and Walt Poole behind. There was another Weatherford rider south of him but he did not know this. Nor was it important. He could not rush ahead or sneak backwards.

Walt would shoot the man the moment he got into a position where it would be possible for him to do it. Bill knew this. He felt no sympathy

111

for the bushwhacker, but he did not like the idea of the man being killed like this, so he tried again.

"Hey, Moore — don't get yourself killed for nothing. I'm in front, Walt's behind. Step out of there without your gun."

The bushwhacker came out, but not as Bill had told him to. For two seconds Bill saw the man's narrow, long face, the too-close, ferret-like pale eyes, and before he could decide that this one and Rob Moore looked very much alike, the bushwhacker fired at Bill's tree without lifting his sixgun from belly-level. Bark and splinters flew. Bill instinctively winced, then he heard the man charging at him, sucked still farther around his tree, got belly-down, raised his cocked Colt, held his breath, and the first glimpse he had of soiled, faded clothing, he fired upwards.

The bushwhacker seemed not to have been hit, but he turned in a twisting way toward Bill. Still with his sixgun held low, he fired, and within a fraction of a second fired again. He was incredibly fast at cocking and firing a Colt. The first bullet missed Bill by inches, the second one made a searing flash of fire pass down his right leg. Then Bill fired his second shot, and that time impact did what the bullet had not been able to do, it knocked the bushwhacker backwards until his legs became entangled. He struck a tree as he was falling, but still got off his third shot, and again the musty needles and ancient dust exploded less than two inches from Bill's face.

Bill felt water flooding into his eyes as he fired his final shot. He missed. The bushwhacker was already going down. He fell forward on his face.

Bill was blinking rapidly when he cocked his Colt. There was pungent gunsmoke through the area of tall trees, and there were diminishing echoes, but no more gunfire.

Walt Poole appeared in full view, but with his knees sprung for springing clear. He too was holding a cocked sixgun as he came close and stared at the downed man, then turned toward Bill.

"You all right?"

Bill eased down the hammer, twisted to run his right hand down his leg, and brought it back up streaked with blood. "I guess I'm not all right," he told Walt Poole.

Eleven

Dawn

Jess and Bud Fisk did not appear east of the punky deadfall until Walt and his companion had sliced Bill's trouser-leg to make a bandage. The wound was not serious; it was about eight inches long though, and bled freely until Walt got that stopped with one of his shirt-tail bandages. Once, the younger cowboy glanced up at Bill and said, "If you'd moved your head he'd have got you through the skull."

Bill did not comment, neither did Walt Poole. When he had finished bandaging the injured leg and leaned to arise, Jess and Bud walked up. One of them was carrying a carbine, the other one had an ivory-stocked sixgun shoved into the waistband of his britches. They soberly watched Walt Poole stand up; when he did this they could see Bill's bandaged leg. Bud looked down. "Bad, Bill?" he asked, and the rangeboss shook his head. "Naw, but it could have been. That man lyin' over yonder is the sharpshooter." Bill's gaze did not leave the face-down dead man. "I was lucky as hell.

That's all it was — luck." He turned back toward Fisk. "Where's the other one?"

"Dead. He was tryin' to free the horses and set us afoot." Bud touched the ivory-stocked Colt in his waistband. "This belonged to him." As he said this he half turned, and Rob Moore saw the ivory-handled Colt. He let his breath out slowly while staring at the gun.

For no particular reason the younger man who had been with Walt Poole wrinkled his brows as he looked up through tree-tops, and said, "It's goin' to rain."

Any other time this would not have earned even a skyward glance, but now it did. Bill lifted his face. "We better get this over with; where's that lariat I dropped when the shootin' started?"

Jess had heard little of the discussion over where Bill was sitting. He had been standing with his head turned and slightly lifted. Now, he turned and said, "Riders coming."

They all glanced at Jess. He made an arm gesture indicating the south-west, back in the direction of the distant stage-road. Bud Fisk turned first to glance at the rangeboss, and Bill Burton had a closed-down look on his face. He said nothing, but held out a hand for Bud to assist him in arising. When he was upright there was a shadow of pain in his eyes, but all he said was: "Just like the cavalry — whoever it is, they get here too late."

Bud watched Rob Moore, who was sitting up again, his back to the punky old deadfall. For him, at least, riders were arriving in the nick of time.

Walt strolled down through the trees and watched a band of riders which he originally thought were the Brewster ranch crew, but when they were about a mile out and coming across that swale where the bay horse had been he made a different judgement. They were not rangemen.

Bud walked down there too, made a smoke and quietly studied the riders. "Townsmen," he announced, and Walt inclined his head.

There were six of them, all armed with saddle-guns as well as beltguns, and several of them were bundled inside sheep-pelt coats although it was not as cold now as it had been. In fact, probably as a result of that lingering overcast, it was warmer than it ordinarily would have been this early in the day.

One rider pushed ahead when Walt and Bud stepped away from their trees where they could be seen. The riders dropped to a steady walk, and when the burly man got up close enough to wave with a gloved hand, he called out.

"Did you get 'em?"

Bud spat and turned away as Walt answered. For some reason that question had irritated Bud. "Yeah," called back Walt. "Two dead, one prisoner — and one of your town possemen killed."

The riders came up the slope, solemn and a little wary, then halted. Before a conversation could begin Bud said, "Come along; the boss is back through here."

They worked their way among the trees to the place where Bill was using a crooked tree limb to lean upon. They halted and gazed around. Bill's trouser-leg was stiffening with drying blood; the men who had remained back with Bill had carried the three dead men in, and now had them lying flat out side by side. For a while nothing was said. The riders looked from the bodies to the rumpled, unshaven, sunken-eyed, soiled men who were standing with Bill Burton. Finally, that stocky man said, "I'm George Fuller, and you'll be Bill Burton, rangeboss for Weatherford."

Bill nodded. He knew who George Fuller was; they were acquainted, but that was all. Fuller was the individual who had been opposing George Kimball in the election. He was wearing Kimball's dull old nickel badge.

Fuller looked around again before saying, "That feller you sent back to look after George — he said a lot of things that I couldn't exactly make out."

Burton leaned on his stick gazing at the townsmen. "Plenty of time for talk when we get down out of here. I got a sore leg and all of us are hungry and wore down." He did not say it irritably, but the look in his eyes left no doubt but that the words of the man wearing the badge had not set well with him.

Fuller swung briskly to the ground. "Let's get the horses," he told his companions, who were reasonably fresh and energetic. The Weatherford rangemen made no move to help. They stood like scarecrows watching Fuller head out through the trees. One of the younger riders said, "We're goin' to be short a horse — that one which run off when the posseman got shot."

Walt had a dry solution to that. "It don't matter to dead men if they ride all the way back belly-down behind someone's saddle."

Rob Moore was sitting now with his long legs pulled up, both arms encircling his knees, oblivious to everything which was being said and done.

Bill limped over and poked him with his improvised crutch. "You're a lucky son of a bitch," Bill said shortly.

They exchanged a long look with the other Weatherford riders looking on, then Moore made a dispirited answer. "I'll tell you something, rangeboss. I told Harry and Joe that if we did it — found Paul and killed him — it was goin' to cause more trouble than it'd solve."

"You were right," stated Bill, his tone softening very little. "They should have listened to you."

"I didn't say we shouldn't do it, rangeboss, and I was as willin' as they were, but I figured killin' Paul would be a beginnin' not an ending." For a moment Moore sat gazing upwards, then he also said, "You'll play hell lynchin' me now, won't you?"

Bill nodded because he had been thinking of this when Jess had first detected the sounds of oncoming horsemen. "Yeah. Now we'll let the law do it."

"The law ain't goin' to do it, rangeboss. I didn't kill anyone."

Bill chose not to argue about this. He raised his head as George Fuller and his possemen returned leading the horses. Rob Moore suddenly said, "One question, rangeboss. Would you have hanged me?"

The reply he got was short and brusque. "In a damned minute!"

George Fuller was a little officious, and that annoyed the Weatherford riders, who had been without sleep, food, or rest since the day before. When Fuller swung up and gestured for everyone else to do the same, Walt Poole smiled without a shred of humour and gestured. "Go on, mister. Just take these dead fellers with you. When we get around to it we'll head on back."

Fuller regarded the lanky Montanan for a moment without speaking, then looked over Walt's head to Bill. The rangeboss inclined his head without saying a word.

It took a little longer to tie down the carcasses, but after that Fuller wordlessly led his burdened townsmen back toward the swale without speaking another word to the Weatherford riding crew. He had been piqued, Bill and his companions knew it, and this was the first pleasant thing to happen thus far into the new day.

Bill was watching the last of the riders from Ridgefield pass out through the trees when he

119

said, "I thought he was goin' to want us to ride back to town with him."

Jess grinned. "He was, but he thought better of it. Bill, there are still two Brewster horses up on that damned slope somewhere."

Bill turned toward Rob Moore. "Get up. We're goin to back-track your brothers, an' you know the route they used to get over here."

They got astride. Bud and Walt helped boost the rangeboss across leather, and Bill's jaw-muscles rippled as he settled into position. But the tightly bandaged wound did not seem to be leaking, but an occasional drop of blood so all Bill Burton had to suffer through was the discomfort, and for a fact a length of sliced meat on a man's upper leg pained him more with a horse moving under it than a broken arm would have.

Bud was puzzled about one thing; the new lawman from Ridgefield had not taken Rob Moore back with him. He mentioned this to Bill and got a slow answer. Bill looked up to where Moore was riding double with Walt Poole and said, "I think Fuller used to be a rangeman. I heard that somewhere. I got a feelin' he wanted us to take Moore along — an' leave him hangin' from a tree up here somewhere."

Fisk frowned. "You figure to do it?"

"No. Not now. Before they came up I figured to do it, Bud, but not after those five townsmen with Fuller saw Moore with us. Townsmen are gutless when it comes to handin' out justice.

120

They prefer the law — and there isn't hardly any comparison."

They found the horses, not by tracks but because after having been tied to trees under saddle all night they were hungry, and nickered at the first scent of other horses.

They put Rob Moore on one of the stolen animals, and Jess grinned as he flipped a lariat noose around the captive's neck, then rode behind Moore with the slack dallied once around his saddlehorn.

They had to stop four times so Bill could lie down and rest. It was a long ride at best, but under those circumstances they did not even get back onto their own range until afternoon, and did not see Weatherford rooftops until the sun was slanting away and reddening with the approach of day's end.

The *cosinero* was roused from his doze beside Paul Franklyn at the bunkhouse and came forth to look. He did not offer to come down to the barn as the dog-tired men dismounted and led their horses inside to be cared for, but eventually he crossed to the cookshack to fire up his stove.

Bill was ready to go to bed. He had bled some on the ride back, and he was tired all the way through to the bone, but what had sapped him more than anything else was having to fight pain every inch of the way. Something like that drained a man of more than just his vitality.

But he hobbled ahead as they all went to the bunkhouse with Rob Moore; all crowded inside to watch Paul and his cousin confront each other, and only Jess sat down as Moore saw his cousin lying there, alive.

Moore showed nothing on his face as he stood staring. Neither did Paul, who stared straight back. It was Paul who finally broke the silence when he said, "Where are Joe and Harry?"

Moore answered flatly. "Dead." He did not elaborate, and Paul did not push for an explanation. He regarded the fox-faced taller man for a long time before speaking again.

"I didn't murder your paw, Rob. He came out onto the porch. I told him to go back and get his gun. He reached inside and pushed a shotgun straight at me and fired — killed the horse, and I was pinned by one leg. Then he cocked the thing and came at me — and I shot him."

It was quiet enough to hear men breathing. Rob Moore did not shift his eyes from the man in the bunk even for a second. "You had no business over there, Paul. We claimed that range."

"Rob — it is done. What's the sense of talkin' about what happened back yonder? I sure as hell didn't want it to end like this, but it did. Do you figure to keep it alive?"

Rob Moore finally allowed his eyes to shift. He looked around the bunkhouse, then over where a bucket with a dipper-handle sticking up out of it was standing, and limped over there to drink deeply. He did not face his cousin again. When he let the dipper slide back into the bucket he faced Bill Burton. "You still figure to use that lariat rope, rangeboss?"

Bill eased down upon the long bench on the east side of the old bunkhouse table, and only answered after he had done this. "No. The law can have you. But I'm goin' to tell you the same thing Jess told that posseman back up there — the feller your brother shot off his horse — leave it be. Like Paul said, it's done. If you don't leave it be — look around you — every damned one of us will hunt for you, and we'll find you, an' next time it won't be a rope nor a cowtown jailhouse, it'll be a bullet. I give you my word on that."

The fox-faced man said, "It's a private matter, rangeboss."

Walt Poole wagged his head. "You're not goin' to let it be, are you? Mister, you're the only one left an' what the hell did all that ridin' and fightin' do? Got some men killed — two of 'em never even been in the country where you come from. They wasn't any part of your silly damned feud. By my lights, that's not right. You'd ought to be satisfied you fellers was wrong. You'd ought to be satisfied you aren't dead too. What the hell is it goin' to take to make you see it's over and done with?"

If the fox-faced man had an answer he did not get an opportunity to offer it; across the yard, with dusk settling, the *cosinero* was out there on his porch beating the triangle which summoned everyone to supper.

Bill struggled to arise. Bud Fisk frowned at him. "Go to bed. Take a couple swallows of whiskey. I'll bring back some grub and black coffee." He turned and jerked his head at their captive, and half-way across the yard he tapped Moore's arm because he had something to say.

"Maybe they'll hang you for bein' an accessory when Sheriff Kimball got killed, but if they don't, if they send you to prison for a few years, think like you never thought before. There's no way you can win at what you set out to do, an' if you try maybe fifteen, twenty years from now, you'll walk out of prison right square into some-one's bullet. Moore, this is a damned short trip from the saddle to the grave as it is. If you come out of prison when you're about as old as I am — think. Don't waste what's left. Now go on in there and eat."

Twelve

A Visitor

A portly man driving a dusty top-buggy arrived in the yard about an hour after supper, tied up at the barn, brought a little leather satchel with him to the bunkhouse, and looked owlishly around when someone opened the door for him. Then he saw Paul, and after nodding around went over beside the bunk to stand looking down.

"I'm Doc Evans," he told Franklyn.

Walt made one of his barbed, dry remarks. "You're a little late, ain't you, Doc? That feller was shot day before yestiddy."

Doctor Evans turned a dispassionate gaze upon Walt, then yanked an old chair around to sit down beside Paul's bunk. He was a moon-faced man, perhaps in his early sixties. He had cigar ash on his coat and did not remove his hat as he went to work examining Paul's wound. But he was efficient. When he made a fresh bandage, he washed the swollen, bluish flesh first, then doused it with a white powder which stung, and as he worked his mouth was flattened, his eyes stone-steady with concentration, while his large, fleshy hands went about their undertaking with absolute confidence.

When he had finished and straightened up he looked at Paul and said, "You'll be all right. Maybe in a month you'll be back to work. In a couple of weeks you'll be able to ride a little. If you got a lick of sense you'll take things slow and easy for about a month, though — but I've never yet met a rangeman I gave this advice to who followed it." He did not smile as he arose and looked around at the other men. "Where is the rangeboss?"

Jess jerked a thumb toward the little door which led into Bill Burton's room. With a curt nod toward Jess the portly medicine practitioner picked up his little satchel and crossed the room. He somehow or other exuded an impression that rangemen were not his favourite people, and after he had closed the door behind him and disappeared into the rangeboss's quarters, Walt said, "I wonder what it'd take to make a human bein' out of him?"

But with the door closed at his back, facing the bunk where Bill Burton was lying with an empty dish and coffee-cup beside him, the doctor looked longest at the half-empty whiskey-bottle, then walked over, hooked his thumbs into vest pockets and regarded Burton as he said, "You're a little long in the tooth for charging all over the country shooting at people."

Bill pointed. "Pull up that chair, Frank. It's

just a cut. I'll live. Did you look at the kid out yonder?"

The portly man was dragging the chair over when he replied. "Yes. And I also saw that rat-faced man you have chained to a bunk." Doctor Evans sat down and this time he removed his hat, then reached for the whiskey-bottle. As he raised it he said, "It'll be cold riding back tonight," and took two big swallows before offering the bottle to Bill.

The rangeboss refused. "I already drank enough. I can just barely find my butt with both hands." He watched the portly man put the bottle aside. "Did you look at those two dead men Fuller brought back with him?"

"Three dead men, Bill. You mean the two strangers?"

"Yes."

"I looked at them. They're in my embalming-shed out back. What about them?"

"Nothing. I shot one of them. He'd be the feller with the hole through his chest. He's the one that shot the kid in the other room, and I'm sure he's also the man who killed George Kimball."

The medical man pulled up his sleeves and leaned. "I'm going to cut the rest of that trouser-leg. Now lie still." As he worked the portly man spoke quietly. "Ridgefield is up in arms. The Town Council appointed Fuller to fill out George's term, and since there was only those two running for sheriff he'll keep the job. Well, it's a messy wound. Where is the water-bucket?"

"Over by the stove."

Doctor Evans brought the bucket over, sat down again with a grunt and said, "What are you going to do with that rat-faced man, Bill?"

"Wait for Fuller. He'll probably be out in the morning."

"Bill, if Fuller takes that man back to town they'll lynch him as sure as I'm sitting here."

Bill's jaw-muscles bunched a little as the doctor began cutting ragged flesh. Through closed teeth he said, "I don't care if they do. I might even donate a new length of rope."

"Do you want another swallow of whiskey?"

"No. What the hell are you doing, Frank?"

"Before I stitch it I've got to scissor off the ragged pieces of loose meat. I'll be through in a minute."

"You sure that boy out in the other room will be all right?"

"Yes. Here, take another swallow. I'm going to sew it up."

Bill obeyed, handed back the bottle and looked up at the large man. "Wait a minute with that damned needle. You remember my little boy?"

"Yes."

"He'd be about that feller's age by now."

Doctor Evans was fishing in his coat for a steel case which contained his glasses. He put the glasses on and pushed them up his nose, then sat for a long while gazing at Bill Burton. He did not say anything though, until he started to lean over again, with the threaded needle poised like a javelin. "Is he a good hand, Bill?"

"For someone no older than he is, he's real good with livestock."

"Then keep him on the ranch. Now hold still, this will hurt a little."

Each time he completed a suture Doc Evans grunted. That was how Bill knew that he had put eight of them in his wound. When the job had been completed Frank Evans leaned back and heaved a big sigh. "This is going to keep you off a horse for at least a month, Bill."

"How about a wagon?"

Frank Evans's pale eyes showed exasperation. "Hell yes, Bill, climb up into a wagon in a few days — bust the damned stitches open. You can always get me back out here to patch you up again — unless of course you get the leg infected, catch blood poisoning in it, then you won't need me, you'll need the preacher."

Frank Evans washed in the bucket, snapped his little satchel closed, and went to work preparing the wound for the bandaging he had placed close at hand. His face was red and shiny in the lamplight.

Bill could feel the pain and he could also feel the effects of the whiskey he had consumed. One did not cancel out the other but it made it harder to concentrate on feeling pain. He said, "A damned month."

Doctor Evans did not reply until he had finished bandaging the leg and had leaned back again. Being a thick, heavy man, working sitting down in a leaning-forward position caused him discomfort. Now that he was finished he could draw a deep breath and relax. He looked at Burton, dug out two cigars, lighted one for himself and handed the other one to Bill, then helped him light it.

"A month," he said thoughtfully, then he removed his cigar and considered the evenly burning tip of it. "Bill?"

"Yes."

"That other one, the one chained to his bunk — he is about the age your son would have been too."

Burton lay looking straight up with fragrant cigar smoke rising from his face as the medical man arose, adjusted his coat, picked up the little satchel and stood gazing down. Bill finally spoke in a flat tone of voice.

"There would not have been any comparison, Frank."

Doctor Evans did not dispute this, except to say, "How do you know that? There probably would not have been, Bill, but how do you know? From what I heard in town this one you have chained and the other two were trying to avenge their father."

"Frank, you don't know the whole story."

"I don't have to know the whole story, Bill. That's not what we're discussing. How do you know your boy would not have ridden an identical trail if someone had shot you down? Those things never have to be justified, Bill, they simply have to happen."

The rangeboss did not look at Frank Evans or open his mouth, so the medical practitioner went to the door, held the latch in his hand as he looked thoughtfully back, and said, "One month, and if you bust those stitches open and I have to drive out here again — the price will be twenty dollars instead of two. Good night."

The portly doctor nodded to the seated men as he passed through the bunkhouse, then out front, down by the barn where his rig was standing, he encountered Bud Fisk, who had watered, trained and hayed the buggy-mare. Bud was leaning on the rack smoking a cigarette and turned slowly as the doctor approached. They nodded, the doctor looked at his old mare, who was still chewing, and smiled. "I'm obliged to you for looking after her," he said.

Bud trickled smoke, eyeing the portly man. "Someone had to, Doctor, and it didn't look like you was goin' to. How's Bill?"

Frank Evans flushed in the darkness when he replied a trifle shortly. "I have a feed-bag under the seat. I always grain her before we start back. Bill will be fine if he stays off a horse, avoids heavy lifting, and uses the leg just to keep it exercised, but not for anything else. It will take a month to heal enough so he can ride again."

"And the kid, Doctor?"

Doctor Evans studied Bud Fisk's bronzed,

hatbrim-shadowed face. "The same length of time, about a month. His wound is more serious but he's a lot younger. That makes a difference." Doctor Evans drew down a deep breath and then said, "If you fellers hand that sharp-faced man over to Sheriff Fuller, and he takes him to town tomorrow, they'll lynch him. The place is in a violent mood over George Kimball's killing."

"Did you tell this to Bill?"

"Yes. He'll send him in anyway."

"Well, Doctor, the son of a bitch won't be any loss," stated Bud, and dropped his smoke to stamp on it. "Kimball is dead, isn't he, and so is another of the townsmen."

The portly man leaned across the back of his buggy-mare. "You're the tophand, aren't you — Fisk?"

"Yes."

"I'd like to ask you a question, Mister Fisk."

"Shoot."

"Did that man in the bunkhouse kill George Kimball?"

"I wasn't there, Doctor, I don't know. But we got a feelin' it was one of the others; one of 'em could shoot the whiskers off a gnat at fifty yards."

"Then why are you men willing to see this one lynched?"

"He was there, Doctor. He was one of them."

Frank Evans continued to lean, gazing over at Bud. He did not say a word for a long time, then he stepped back, climbed into his rig, backed

132

clear, turned the mare and drove out of the yard.

Bud continued to lean on the tie-rack until the top-buggy disappeared in the darkness, and for a while afterwards. Eventually he went to the bunkhouse, shed his boots, hat, vest and gun-belt, and was about to sit down on his bunk to tug off his britches when he stopped moving, stood a while gazing at the door into the range-boss's room and finally padded over there, rattled the latch, was gruffly told to enter, and did so.

Bill was leaning over to stub out a cigar. The room smelled strongly of stogie-smoke, which was not an unpleasant aroma. Bill looked across the room. "Well, Bud?"

"If that tinhorn sheriff comes out tomorrow to haul Moore back with him, are you goin' to hand Moore over?"

Bill groaned and eased back down on his bunk, looking straight up. "Not tomorrow. Maybe in a week, but not tomorrow. They're goin' to have themselves one of those bonfire lynchings if Fuller takes him back tomorrow. Give 'em a week or two to calm down. Why?"

Bud reached behind for the door-latch, and squeezed it. "Nothing. Good night."

Burton turned as the tophand was opening the door. *"Why?"*

Bud hesitated with the ajar door at his back, and smiled a little. "I didn't think you'd do that. I just wanted to be sure I was right. Good night."

Burton remained in his awkwardly leaning

posture until the door was closed, then he tried to reach the whiskey-bottle. It was about four inches beyond his straining hand. He moved his lower body slightly to gain ground, and pain shot upwards from his injured leg, which was not only swollen but which was more painful now after Doctor Evans had patched it than it had been before.

He said, "Damn it all," and eased back down upon the bunk.

Out front, in the big main room of the bunkhouse, there was not a sound. It was not really very late; under most circumstances someone would have dug out the old greasy set of bunkhouse cards and talked up a poker session. Tonight, the Angel Gabriel could have materialised packing a sack of gold coins and a new deck of cards and none of the rangecrew would even have lifted their heads to look.

The last lamp to be turned out was across the yard at the cookshack where the *cosinero* had finished peeling two dozen spuds which he would slice up and fry along with steaks, for breakfast, and he was contentedly humming to himself. There was flour up one of his arms.

Three men did not go directly to sleep, although they were dead-tired. One was Rob Moore, who had seen his two brothers killed today, another was Bud Fisk, who was solemnly looking at the slats of the bunk above his bunk, and the third man was Bill Burton, also lying in darkness wide awake.

134

Thirteen

Angry Men

It was raining in the morning, not heavily but steadily, and evidently it had been raining most of the night because the yard and all the rooftops were soaked. It had been a while since the last rainfall, the earth and rooftops were as dry as cotton, so it required considerable water to make them show run-off.

The *cosinero* was in a grumbly mood when he fixed three separate platters of grub for Bud and Jess to take back with them to the bunkhouse. He said Weatherford had turned from a respectable cow outfit to a damned home for wrecked individuals. Neither Bud nor Jess argued, although neither one was above growling back when someone disparaged the ranch or the rangeboss. Outside, Jess said, "Give him an hour. He'll be smiling again. He ain't been to the flour-barrel yet."

Bud frowned. "Is that where he keeps it hid?"

Jess was a shrewd, wizened man. "I've noticed over the past year or so that whenever he's got flour on his right arm he's in a good mood. When he ain't, he's in a bad mood."

Bud thought that over, then laughed just before they entered the bunkhouse. He was still amused when he set the food on a horse-shoe keg beside Paul Franklyn's bunk, and Paul leaned for the coffee-cup as he said, "I'm getting saddle-sores."

Bud shook water off his hat. "The doctor said you'd be out of things for about a month."

Paul stopped, reached and stared upwards. "A month! I'm ready to get out of this bed right now."

"You *think* you are, partner." Bud put a hard look downward. "You're goin' to stay in the bunk until Bill or I tell you to get out of it."

There was an unrelenting look on the top-hand's face. Paul picked up the coffee-cup and leaned back again.

Bud took his second platter on through to Bill Burton's room, and in there at least he got no argument about arising. Bill's leg was not only very painful, it was even more swollen than it had been yesterday. About the only way Bill Burton would have considered getting out of his bunk was if the bunkhouse caught fire.

Bud laced his hot coffee with whiskey and put the cup and platter on a box beside the bunk. As he straightened back he said, "It's comin' down out there. I expect we might as well grease wagons today, patch harness and whatnot, eh?"

Bill looked at the food. He had not been hungry, but now he was, and gritted his teeth as

136

he jockeyed up onto one elbow. "How's the kid?"

"Wants to get up."

Bill's brows dropped. "He stays in that bunk!"

"I told him that. How are you this morning?"

"Sore as hell. Every time Frank does somethin' to me I feel worse'n I'd felt before."

"That's a hell of a lookin' leg, Bill."

"Pour some more whiskey in this coffee, Bud."

After the tophand had obeyed, he held up the bottle. There was not much left. "You're goin' to be out soon." He put the bottle down and said, "You want anything? If not I'll take the crew down to the wagon-shed and the barn. If it don't let up by this afternoon we might as well shoe some of the using horses too."

Bill finished the laced coffee and was hungrier than before. He was beginning to eat when he said, "Yeah," and that was all he had to say so Bud returned to the outer room where the men were waiting. He sent them to the barn and shed with orders, then turned towards Rob Moore, who was watching him with that ferret-like crafty expression he showed occasionally.

There was nothing about Rob Moore that Bud Fisk liked. He strolled over and leaned on a nearby bunk as he said, "You need to go out back to the outhouse?"

Moore shook his head. Jess and Walt had already taken him back there. "I'm out of smokin' tobacco," he said, and Bud tossed his own two-thirds full sack onto the bunk where Moore was trace-chained. Then Moore said, "I been thinking about what you told me in the yard last night. I got a hunch you're right. It's over."

Bud straightened up with a little nod of his head, and walked out of the bunkhouse. As he was passing Paul's bunk near the door he winked.

It was awkward in the bunkhouse. Paul and his cousin were alone, neither spoke to the other although both were acutely conscious of the other. Eventually Moore made a remark which was contrary to the impression he had left with Bud Fisk.

"Don't nobody get out of somethin' like this as easy as you been doing, Paul."

Franklyn gazed diagonally over where Moore was chained to a bunk. He did not speak for a while because it troubled him to realise what he should have realised earlier; Rob Moore was still the most underhanded of the three Moore boys, the sneakiest and most cunning and sly, and he had known all this from early childhood. But after what had happened yesterday, and after the way Rob had been acting since he'd been at the ranch, Paul had begun to believe Rob had come to accept what everyone else already knew. It *was* the end of the feud.

When Paul remained silently looking over at him, Rob Moore spoke again. "An' they ain't takin' me to some cowtown to be lynched, neither."

Paul still said nothing. A gradual feeling of suspicion formed in his mind. Rob had always been devious, shrewd and untrustworthy. Ever since they had been children Rob had said one thing and had done something different; he was completely unscrupulous, and he had also been generally unpredictable.

But Moore said no more. He slyly smiled at his cousin, and leaned back to get comfortable on the bunk. He was still craftily smiling when Paul said, "I don't know that the law'd let folks lynch you."

Without losing his death's-head grin Moore answered shortly. "We killed that gawddamned sheriff, didn't we?" Then he brought his close-set eyes down. "Paw used to say if you set any man on a good horse there wasn't anything folks could do to him, if he knew enough to keep clear of 'em."

Paul let his breath out silently. He did not see any connection with his cousin's present situation and what Rob's father had said. He turned up onto his uninjured side so he would not have to look across the room, and outside someone angrily shouted something which only carried as an angry sound into the bunkhouse. The words were indistinguishable. But Paul recognised the bull-bass voice. It belonged to the ranch cook.

Again the *cosinero* shouted from the porch of his cookshack, and this time a wiry, short man with bowed legs appeared opposite him in the barn doorway. "What are you hollerin' about?" Jess called out.

He got an immediate retort. "Some sneakin' louse been in my flour-barrel!"

Jess considered that, then said, "What of it? Maybe someone needed a handful of flour to make paste with. Why get all fired up over a little flour?"

The *cosinero* stood in red-faced wrath glaring over at the front of the barn. He was ready to choke, but he did not speak again. If he had, he would have revealed his secret. A big vein throbbed at his temple. He turned abruptly and flung inside, slamming the door after himself.

Jess turned back where the men were doubled over in silent mirth, and Bud Fisk, holding a half-full bottle of rye whiskey with flour like dust still on it, said, "If he'd had a gun he'd have shot you, Jess."

The wiry man was unimpressed. "He couldn't hit the broad side of a barn from the inside. You better go out the back way to Bill's room with that bottle, and hide it inside your shirt."

Walt Poole wiped his eyes with a soiled sleeve. "If he'd caught you in there diggin' in that flour barrel, Jess, he'd have busted you in half."

Jess was still unimpressed as he said, "You never saw me run when I was scairt, Walt. He couldn't have even got close."

That started the laughter again. Jess turned to walk back for another look across the yard, and stopped dead-still near the doorway. Through the drizzling mist a band of riders was approaching. They looked like ghosts and did not make a sound on the sodden ground. Without turning he called to Fisk.

"Bud! It's the law from town!"

Fisk put the whiskey-bottle on a shelf among liniment bottles, and they all walked up to look. The bull-built squatty man in the lead would have been recognizable even if he hadn't pinned George Kimball's old badge on the outside of his shiny-wet black slicker. There were five bunched-up riders with him, each one with a Winchester slung under his saddle-fender. They were still a fair distance out and were riding at a walk, but just looking out there was enough; Sheriff Kimball's successor was not going to be ordered away this time. Yesterday, up where the killings had occurred, he had not been quite sure of himself. This morning he was, and it showed as he rode steadily closer to the soggy big ranch-yard.

Bud started for the bunkhouse without a word. The other men remained in the doorway watching those wet-shiny possemen until Walt dryly said, "What in hell did he need an army for, just to take back one unarmed man?"

Jess and Bud Fisk had talked together out back. Jess now said, "Bill ain't goin' to hand Moore over."

All the men looked at Jess, who was still watching the oncoming riders. A young cowboy said, "Why not, Jess?"

141

"Because they'll Lynch him in town."

The younger cowboy scowled. "We'd have done it yesterday. What's the difference — up there or over in Ridgefield?"

Jess had no answer so he said, "Bill told Bud we'd keep the bastard around for a week or two, until the folks in town got over howlin' for blood for George Kimball."

No one spoke after that. They turned back to watching the sheriff and his riders, hatbrims dripping, horses plodding ahead less mindful of being soaked than their riders were, none of them making a sound until they came around from behind the cookshack, and entered the yard. Then Sheriff Fuller aimed for the rack out front of the barn, halted, sat a moment gazing at the expressionless rangemen in the big doorway, then eased forward to swing off as he said, "Where's Bill Burton?"

Walt Poole jerked his head. "At the bunk-house."

No one stepped out there to assist with the horses as the possemen dismounted. Sheriff Fuller sensed veiled hostility and scowled at the rangemen, but turned and strode to the bunk-house porch where he shed his poncho, beat water from his hat, then walked inside.

Bud was waiting in the open doorway of the rangeboss's room. He nodded, but that was all, and when Fuller scowled at Rob Moore then said, "Get your hat and coat," before he saw the trace-chain, Fisk spoke quietly.

142

"Bill's in here, Sheriff."

The lawman entered Burton's room, eyed the man on the bunk and seemed to grudgingly say he was sorry to find the rangeboss bad off. Fuller was indeed different than he had been yesterday. He had reason to be different; the entire town of Ridgefield was behind him, and half the men over there had volunteered to ride out to the Weatherford outfit with him.

Bill propped himself up. He put a steely look upon the lawman. "What do you want?" he asked curtly.

Fuller was surprised. The veiled hostility he had seen at the barn was not at all veiled in the rangeboss's room. But Fuller recovered quickly. "That man you got chained to his bunk. You know that, Mister Burton."

Bill did not blink. "He stays here for a week or two. You're not goin' to take him to Ridgefield so's they can have a big bonfire tonight, and lynch the bastard."

Fuller's eyes widened slightly. For a moment he seemed at a loss for words, then his temper came up. "He don't stay here! He's goin' back with us! I'm the law now, Mister Burton. That man's responsible for two good men bein' killed. He's goin' to stand trial as soon as I can find a judge and get him over to Ridgefield."

Bill sneered. "Trial my butt! He'll be dead by tomorrow morning and you know it. In a couple of weeks maybe he could stand trial. Not today, and sure as hell not tonight."

Sheriff Fuller turned toward Bud. The top-hand was standing in a slouch by the door, arms crossed, looking and listening. He showed nothing on his face and looked steadily back at the lawman. Fuller swung back to face the rangeboss again, and now he was angry.

"Mister Burton, I got a posse with me, an' I got a signed warrant for Moore in my office back in town."

"You should have brought it with you," Bill said.

"I didn't figure I'd need it. And by gawd I don't need it. I got the legal authority to arrest that son of a bitch and take him back. Mister Burton, if you interfere, I got the authority to take you an' everyone who resists me back too — under arrest for interferin' with a lawman durin' the performance of his job."

Bill did not yield. "He stays. Sheriff, nobody on the ranch wants to oppose you. What we want is for enough time to pass so's when you do take Moore to Ridgefield he'll live to stand trial. Then — if the law hangs him, fine, but there won't be a lynching."

The angry lawman said, "What in hell do you think I let you have him yesterday for?"

Bill nodded over that. "I knew why you did it. And I'm not goin' to say it wasn't in my mind. But today things are different. Sheriff, don't make a fight out of this."

"By gawd, are you threatenin' me, Mister Burton?"

Bill gently wagged his head. "No — but it's goin' to come to that if you try to take —"

"Bill," Bud Fisk suddenly said, interrupting the rangeboss. "Suppose we take Moore to town and help Sheriff Fuller lock him in a cell, then just sort of set around inside the jailhouse. There'll be some other stockmen over there. They could sort of set around in there with us."

It was a compromise. Both Bill Burton and the sheriff looked at Bud. He was uncomfortable under their stares so he gave his shoulders a little self-conscious shrug and added a little more.

"They can't take him if we won't let 'em do it, Bill, but I got a bad feelin' Mister Fuller'll be back tonight with a lot more townsmen, if we keep Moore here."

Fuller seemed about to spiritedly confirm this, when a sharp, hard voice from the outer room called through the open doorway. Rob Moore said, "That'll work, rangeboss. Get some stockmen to guard me in his damned jailhouse. That'll work; ain't no townsmen got guts enough to storm a jailhouse for a lynchin' if it's full of armed rangemen."

Bill lost some of his rock-hard stubborn look. Sheriff Fuller cleared his throat and seemed uncertain. He would not look at Burton, but scowled at Bud Fisk. Bud, who had not expected anything like the support of the bushwhacker, waited for one of the older men to speak.

Bill finally did, bitterly and grudgingly. "Bud, have the light wagon filled with straw and put a

145

couple of ponchos in it."

For the first time Fisk showed indignation. "What the hell are you talking about! You can't go, Bill, not in your shape, and it's still rainin' out there, you could take a cold in that leg." Bud was standing fully erect, glaring at the range-boss.

Sheriff Fuller broke in. "Put blankets in the wagon too, Mister Fisk. Make him up a dry pallet. He'll be all right. It's only maybe ten miles."

Bud looked at the sheriff, and thought Fuller did not care whether Bill got sicker as a result of something like this. "You keep out of this," he snapped.

Fuller did not open his mouth, but Bill Burton did.

"Bud, make a dry bed in the wagon. I'm goin' along if I got to walk!"

"Doc Evans will —"

"Frank Evans can go to hell," Bill exclaimed. "Go get things ready. If we stand around here arguin' much longer it won't even be daylight by the time we reach Ridgefield. Bud — damn it all — do what I say!"

Fisk's idea of a compromise had back-fired. He was facing two men who had been at each other's throats moments before, and now they were lining up together against him.

He turned and stamped angrily out of the bunkhouse.

Fourteen

Through the Mist

The drizzle had not relented, but it still lacked a lot of being in the same category of rainfall as had fallen last night. Only Jess and one of the younger riders was not upset about the range-boss making the trip in the light wagon, and they were the men charged with preparing a decent straw pallet for Bill, and making it as waterproof as they could. Jess was nearly twice the age of the man helping him; he had been through equivalent situations before and knew what to do. The younger rider learned a lot that morning about how to keep someone dry in an open wagon during a rainfall.

When the riding crew was saddled up and ready to ride — inside the barn because no one liked a wet saddle-seat — Sheriff Fuller and Bud Fisk emerged from the bunkhouse with the bushwhacker. He had been furnished an old poncho to keep him dry, and the chain had been left behind on the bunkhouse porch. Moore did not seem worried, he seemed preoccupied as he limped toward the barn. Fuller's possemen were doing their best to dry off their saddle-seats and scarcely looked at Rob Moore.

Walt drove the light buggy to the bunkhouse door while Jess and one of the younger riders went inside to carry Bill out and get him settled inside a bedroll covered with waterproof canvas, and two black ponchos. He did not say a word, not even after Bud emerged from the barn and signalled for Sheriff Fuller and his townsmen to head out.

The ground was not as hard and bumpy as it would have been if it had been dry, and that helped, but Bill was still in pain. Bud reined over and leaned from the saddle to hand him something. Rainwater had washed off all traces of the flour, but it was the same bottle Jess had stolen from the flour-barrel, and Bill forced a tough smile as he accepted the bottle.

Sheriff Fuller did the customary thing with his horseback-prisoner; he dabbed a little noose around Rob Moore's neck and allowed enough slack so that the prisoner could ride ahead of him in comfort, but there were two dallies around Fuller's saddlehorn; if Moore tried to break clear and run for it all Sheriff Fuller had to do was set up his horse and hold his dallies. Moore would be jerked backwards off the horse, and very probably his neck would be broken.

The drizzle created an unusual mist. It was as though they were all riding through a fallen cloud. They could see no more than perhaps a hundred yards ahead. And yet it was not cold, so they did not have to worry about the rangeboss in that respect. None of them were as knowledgeable about something like this as Doctor Evans was, but Frank Evans was not along so nothing was said, except now and then when a rider would ease up beside the wagon and look at Bill, or try to cheer him up with a joke. Walt Poole, on the buggy-seat, hunched inside his old black poncho like a predatory scarecrow, borrowed a chew from Bill Burton's plug, and kept his head tipped a little so rainwater would drip down in front, and not down his neck in back.

There was every reason to believe that what lay ahead was a somewhat dismal, unreal ride through ghostly, misty rainfall, until they eventually reached Ridgefield.

Bud and Jess were riding stirrup, scarcely speaking. Up ahead, behind the sheriff, his possemen were equally as quiet and slouchful, water dripping from their booted ankles, their carbine-boots partially full of the stuff, their clammy half-dried saddle-seats inhibiting them from conversation or, for that matter, much interest in either their purpose, their destination, or their surroundings.

They covered two miles, could no longer see the Weatherford buildings, and were settling into a routine. The rangemen did not ride up near the possemen, and the townsmen did not heed the rangemen behind them. That hostility back in the yard had made fraternization unlikely, and the dismal weather had added a further inhibiting factor.

Jess looked from beneath his down-tipped hatbrim and said, "Bud, if we'd done what we'd ought to have done yestiddy, we wouldn't be out here gettin' our chingalees wet today."

Bud thought about his reply to that. Jess knew perfectly well why they could not have hanged Rob Moore yesterday, after all those townsmen saw him with them, alive. "If you get your chingalee wet it might grow and that'd enhance your standin' the next time you go to town, Jess."

The smaller man turned his dripping hatbrim. "What does that mean?"

"What?"

"Enhance."

Bud sought the words to use in explaining, and Sheriff Fuller far ahead handed the Turk's head end of his lariat to one of the townsmen, then swung out and around to ride down to the wagon. Bud watched Fuller ease up and lean to look in at Bill Burton. He heard the lawman say, "Mister Burton, I'm sorry we had a disagreement."

Bud was surprised. He would have thought Fuller was not a man to apologise. Fuller's stock rose a notch in Fisk's opinion. Maybe it also did in Bill's estimation because he raised his head up out of his dry place and smiled. "Well hell, Sheriff, men only get to know one another when they disagree a little." Then Bill pulled down a fresh breath of air, and Bud grinned to himself;

for Bill Burton to apologise was like him opening his mouth voluntarily to have some teeth pulled.

"Sheriff, I'm ashamed of myself. But I just didn't want a lynching."

"Mister Burton, take my word for it — there would not have been one."

Up ahead someone let go with a startled shout. Every head back by the wagon raised and swung forward. A horseman was racing belly-down away on an angling, north-easterly course. He was riding so low across the neck of his animal he looked more like a wet-shiny lump than a man. For a hundred yards a long length of rope flopped and snapped in his wake, then it was tossed aside.

Bud Fisk ripped out a curse and went ahead in a wild, lunging run. Jess and the other Weatherford men were slower to understand what had happened, and up ahead, where they were closer, the town possemen were milling like sheep.

Bill yelled at Sheriff Fuller, and the lawman whirled, hooked his horse, which flung mud rearwards, and Fuller too joined the pursuit.

Bill forgot, and started to push upwards in his bedroll, and the pain hit him like the kick of a mule. He sank back gasping and sputtering curses.

Rob Moore's remark to his cousin about a man on a good horse would have made sense right at this moment, if any of the riders pursuing him had heard it. They hadn't, and Paul was still back there in his bunk at the ranch with only an irate *cosinero* for company.

The horse was indeed a good one. It had come from the Weatherford using remuda; Bill never kept any other kind of working horse on the ranch.

Within minutes Bill and Walt were alone. There was a great, straggling gaggle of horsemen running in pursuit of Rob Moore, wet ponchos flopping around each man like a pair of shiny black wings.

Jess was light and he rode even lighter in the saddle. Furthermore, being privileged on the ranch, he chose his own mounts. Now, he passed possemen one at a time until he swerved in very close to the foremost one, leaned and whipped out the man's Winchester, then without even looking at the startled posseman rowelled his horse ahead.

He came up even with Bud Fisk clutching the Winchester, which none of the other Weatherford riders had rigged themselves out with, because at the time they had left the ranch there had been no need for long-range weapons.

Bud turned, saw the gun, and as Jess sped past Bud began to angle slightly to his right, more north-easterly, his clear intention being to force the escaping bushwhacker to hold a steady course while Jess closed up on him a foot at a time. Moore was well mounted but Jess was better mounted.

Moore looked over his hunched shoulder, saw

Jess coming, saw the Winchester, and for a few yards held steadily to his course, then, in sight of all the men farther back, he eased up a little, carefully reined his horse around on the slippery ground, and as Jess slackened off trying to guess what the bushwhacker was doing, Moore turned and rowelled his horse directly at the Weatherford rangeman.

They were not far apart even before Moore turned back. Now, it dawned on Jess that he was no longer being the pursuer, he eased up on the reins to turn slightly away so that he could loop his reins and use both hands on the carbine. He was out-foxed at that too; Moore was straightening up in the saddle. He flung back the loose poncho sleeve of his right hand, and too late Jess saw the little nickel-plated belly-gun with its under-and-over, big-bore muzzles. He grunted in a frantic effort to lean far forward when Moore fired. The bullet raked Jess's back, tearing through the poncho and his shirt and bringing an almost instantaneous rush of blood.

If he had hesitated before leaning, Jess would have been shot through the body and knocked off his horse; the little belly-gun, while it had no appreciable range, fired two .44 calibre slugs. Being struck in the body by a bullet of that size would have knocked down a horse at close range, and Jess did not weigh a hundred and sixty pounds, wringing wet.

Bud was yelling something and spurring to

reach Jess, but despite his haste he was too far away.

Jess cocked the Winchester and fired it wildly with one hand, then leaned all his weight to make the horse beneath him give way, and as the animal did this Jess looped his reins, saw the bushwhacker aiming for his last shot, and Jess fired first, levered up and fired again, then his horse was bearing him beyond belly-gun range. He picked up the reins to wheel back around, saw Bud Fisk cross between them and also saw Bud with his cocked Colt shoulder high, bring his mount into a sliding halt.

Jess did not see the bushwhacker, he only saw the riderless horse go fleeing back in the direction of the oncoming riders. He did not see Rob Moore until he came back at a stiff trot and could ride around Bud Fisk, who was sitting his horse in a slouch.

The bushwhacker was lying on his face in the mud, the shiny old poncho up half-way over his chest, shoulders and head. There was no sign of the derringer until Fisk stiffly dismounted and rolled Rob Moore face up. The little gun was beneath him, and Bud picked it up, held it, and looked around at Jess.

"Are you hit?" he asked.

Jess had a smarting, stinging sensation but no actual pain — yet. "Grazed," he said, balancing the posseman's carbine on his lap. "Where did I hit him?"

Bud pointed with the little gun. "Twice. Once

through the left arm, the second time through the lights."

"Is he dead?"

Bud nodded and faced around as other riders came up flinging mud in their attempt to halt excited animals.

Sheriff Fuller did not hurry after he saw the bushwhacker go off his horse. He trotted up, looked, wordlessly swung to the ground and stepped close to the body and stared bitterly at it.

Bud held out his hand. "Here, take it."

Fuller took the belly-gun and looked again at the dead man. "Where did he get this thing?"

Fisk did not know. "Likely from inside his boot. We didn't search him when we caught him."

Fuller raised his head in Jess's direction. "You all right?"

The pain was finally taking over, and the rainfall spread blood over Jess's back, saddle, and the rump of his horse. Several possemen paled at the gory sight. Jess felt around and did not answer Fuller, he started riding away at a walk, heading in the direction of the wagon where Walt Poole and Bill Burton had witnessed everything from a distance.

Bud swung astride to follow Jess. He said, "You can take the son of a bitch back with you, Sheriff. You won't need us any more."

The other Weatherford riders reined around to follow Bud Fisk. When they reached the wagon Walt had Jess bent over a high rear wheel of the wagon, making a bandage out of Jess's soggy, torn shirt, and Bill Burton was leaning over the sideboards with rain running down his face listening to Walt curse as he tried to staunch the bleeding. Walt bitterly complained that every time some damned idiot got himself hurt they came running to him, and no one ever brought any bandaging material with them.

They eventually put Jess inside the wagon with Bill and turned back toward the ranch. Jess's back pained him, but not so much that he did not remember having seen Bud hand Bill the whiskey-bottle he had stolen from the flour-barrel, so he asked for it.

After that he did not feel much better, but he worried about it less. When he had first realised he had been shot, had felt warm blood flowing from his back, he had thought the wound was worse than it was, and had worried about bleeding to death, which was why he had left the others and had ridden back in search of Walt Poole.

Now, his horse being led by one of the other men, Jess had another couple of pulls at the bottle before Bill took it away from him and shoved it deep into the straw under the bedroll.

They reached the yard with pre-dusk gloom settling over everything, got Jess and Bill to the bunkhouse, then Bud sent a man over to the cookshack with orders for the *cosinero* to make a big kettle of beef broth, and fetch it to the bunkhouse while it was still simmering.

Paul Franklyn listened to the stories and lay silent for a long while. It was Walt, drying his hands on an old soiled towel, who brought Paul out of his silence. Walt said, "He likely had that damned derringer in his boot back up yonder, and was waitin' for a chance to use it, but we were around him all the time, too many of us for a gun that only held two slugs."

Paul looked quietly at Walt Poole. "It wouldn't have made any difference, Walt. With or without his hide-out gun, Rob was not going to make it. He was never going to change. Sooner or later —"

Poole nodded and headed for Jess's bunk where the wizened rangeman was lying on his stomach. Walt had more to work with at the bunkhouse; he was an experienced man at this sort of thing. As he leaned down he said, "Why didn't you shoot when you saw him turnin' around?"

"Because I thought he was figurin' on running into me. I didn't know he had a gun. Hey, what are you puttin' on my back, it burns like hell?"

"Goose grease and alum. It works good at sealin' off the bleedin' on a horse."

"Well, gawddammit, I'm not a horse!"

"Hold still and shut up."

Bud and Bill, in the rangeboss's room with the door partly ajar, were letting a lot of tension ease out as they sat in silence. Then Bud said, "Nothing much to do now for a while anyway,

Bill. The ground won't dry out for a week."

"Yeah."

"The cook will whine around about the bunk-house bein' like a hospital."

"Yeah."

Bud turned. "What's troubling you?"

"I'm trying real hard to feel sorry for that son of a bitch. Anyone who gets themself killed deserves pity."

"Not that one, Bill. Not his brothers either."

Burton sighed. "What happened to that bottle? I left it in the straw under my bedroll."

"I'll go get it."

"Not for me, Bud. Give Paul a couple of pulls off it. Since he's been lyin' here, everything he knew back home came unravelled for him."

"All right," stated the tophand, arising to his feet. At the door he looked back. "He said he likes it here. If a young man's got to begin over, he could do worse."

"I hope he believes that, Bud."

The tophand walked through the outer room, put his hat on and left the bunkhouse, which, for a fact, was beginning to smell like a hospital.

The employees of G.K. Hall hope you have enjoyed this Large Print book. All our Large Print titles are designed for easy reading, and all our books are made to last. Other G.K. Hall books are available at your library, through selected bookstores, or directly from us.

For information about titles, please call:

(800) 257-5157

To share your comments, please write:

Publisher
G.K. Hall & Co.
P.O. Box 159
Thorndike, ME 04986